# SECOND CHANCE IN LAGUNA

## CLAIRE MARTI

CLAIRE MARTI

*To Todd for giving me the space and the confidence to write my first novel all those years ago! I love you so much: you're my ride-or-die.*

# CHAPTER 1

She was not going to scream.

She was not going to scream.

She screamed in sheer frustration.

How could she have misplaced the bloody keys? Sophie muttered as she rummaged through her oversized purse. She just wanted to get inside her new house. Beside her, Zack meowed in agreement.

"I'm sorry, Zack. I'll have you out of the carrier as soon as I find the keys." And now she was talking not only to herself but also to her cat. Not exactly an auspicious beginning to her fabulous new life.

Because it wasn't bad enough traffic had been horrific on Highway 1 driving into Laguna Beach. Nope, then her rear tire decided to explode, and she lost an hour waiting for the AAA man to change it. She white-knuckled it up the narrow, winding road leading to her new home, wincing each time one of the lush green trees scraped against her car.

When a truck materialized around the corner, heading straight for her, she'd swerved and became too familiar with a hedge on the side of Hayden Lane. She thumped her head on the steering wheel, fighting the urge to flip a U-turn, slink back to San Diego with her tail between her legs, and beg for her job back. Hell, beg the universe for her life back.

Now her fresh start was officially a hot mess. She'd plugged her agenda into her calendar, and nowhere did it say risk life and limb on journey or get locked out before actually moving in. She frowned; certain she'd dropped the shiny keys inside her purse when she'd hightailed it out of San Diego this morning.

Fine.

She knelt and dumped the contents of her scarlet satchel onto the quaint porch of her seemingly impenetrable new cottage. Sitting back on her heels, she tossed aside three brand-new lip glosses, some breath mints, an old-fashioned planner, and some stubs from movies she didn't remember attending. What was she doing with all this stuff? Three lip glosses? She only had two lips, for goodness' sake.

No keys.

No way. She never misplaced anything.

Her competence was part of her success as associate editor at *Healthy Woman* magazine. Correction––her former job, as she'd given notice right after her fiancé failed to appear for their wedding. The jerk. She'd shocked her boss, who thought Sophie would throw herself into her work as opposed to shucking it altogether. Maybe this absentmindedness was right in line with her new unemployed status.

Closing her eyes, she inhaled a cleansing breath of the crisp ocean air, hoping for calm to permeate her like it did in yoga class. Inhale and exhale. Everything was going to be okay. Her shoulders softened.

"Bailey, no. Stop," a deep voice shouted.

She glanced up, just in time for one hundred pounds of flying black fur to knock her flat onto her back. An enormous pink tongue slathered her with wet kisses. Laughing, she pushed against the huge paws in a futile attempt to stop the beast that seemed determined to give her face a thorough washing. Her bath ended when someone plucked off her assailant as if she were light as a feather.

"Bad girl, Bailey. Sit. Now." The dog hung her head, attempting to appear ashamed.

"Are you okay?"

Sophie sat up. "Well, I'm certainly clean, but a little surprised by that missile of yours."

The guy extended a strong hand, and she allowed him to pull her to her feet. Awareness prickled along her skin. When she lifted her gaze, her breath lodged in her throat.

For a moment, she was lost in a pair of bottle-green eyes framed with thick dark lashes. Those eyes studied her from a chiseled, square-jawed face that belonged on the cover of GQ magazine. Sun-streaked blond hair fell across his forehead. He was the most beautiful man she'd ever seen.

*No, no, no, remember what the last beautiful man did to you. No men allowed in your new, improved single life.*

"Sophie Barnes?" He quirked an eyebrow.

Her pulse kicked. "I am. And who are you?" She dropped her palm and retreated a step.

*Please don't notice the coffee stains decorating my white tank top.* Another casualty from her trip. She refused to analyze why she cared what he thought.

"I'm Nick Morgan, your landlord. I was just stopping by to make sure you were settling in." He gestured toward the haphazard pile of luggage surrounding her.

"I can't find the keys. I'm not sure where they could be. I know I had them this morning. I never lose things…" She bit her lip.

He waved a hand. "No worries, I'll let you in. Sorry about Bailey. She doesn't have the best manners, but she means well."

At the sound of her name, Bailey thumped her tail and grinned.

"Is she a Lab?" She leaned down to scratch the dog's floppy ears. The tail banged faster.

"Part Lab and part horse. They didn't know when I adopted her at the shelter. All I know is she's failed obedience school twice and doesn't seem to be ashamed of it."

Her shoulders softened. Anyone who rescued animals from the pound had to have at least a partially good heart. She'd rescued Zack from certain death when she found him as a half-starved kitten on the side of the road. He'd become her most loyal and loving companion. The only male she trusted these days.

"Let's get you inside. I'll bring you another set of keys later." Nick unlocked the door, grabbed two of her suitcases, and proceeded inside.

"Great." She stuffed her belongings into her purse and grabbed Zack's carrier.

Gleaming hardwood floors greeted her when she followed him inside. A comfortable overstuffed couch and matching armchair accented by polished teak furniture gave the room a cozy feel. Windows graced every wall, the clear glass shining brightly with the echo of blue skies. Cream crown molding framed walls painted seafoam green. Two arched doorways led from the main room into what appeared to be the kitchen and the bedroom.

"Oh, the photos online didn't do it justice. I love it. It's like a dollhouse." Sophie hummed with pleasure and continued to explore.

A huge four-poster bed with elegant posts soaring up to the high ceiling dominated the bedroom. She stroked her hand along the bed's charming white-lace coverlet. Enormous open windows welcomed in the Southern California sunshine and the ocean breeze.

She continued through a lovely, marble-tiled bathroom into the office, where an old-fashioned rolltop desk faced the window. When she paused to admire the gorgeous view of the Pacific Ocean and clusters of vibrant bougainvillea, Nick's clean, masculine scent reached her nostrils. The hairs on the back of her neck prickled.

Why was he right behind her? "Umm, I should let my cat out of the carrier." She turned and hurried back to the living room.

"Zack, we're home." She unlocked the carrier door, and the cat slinked out, leaped onto the couch, and began washing his peach-colored fur.

Bailey bounded up to greet Zack and licked his face, soaking the cat's head in one stroke. Zack tapped the dog on the nose and moved to higher ground.

Nick laughed, his eyes crinkling at the corners. "Your cat isn't afraid of dogs?"

"Zack isn't afraid of anything, it seems. Don't worry about Bailey."

He ruffled Bailey's fur. "A lot of people are scared of her. She's harmless, just too big for her own good."

"Really? She seems like an adorable goof." Sophie scanned the room again. "The cottage really is charming. Did your wife decorate?" Her gaze flicked down to his left hand. His third finger was bare.

"No wife. My sister just moved out and she's an interior designer. We didn't want it to sit empty." He flashed another sexy grin.

He exuded confidence. Charm. Power. Her stomach flip-flopped.

Damn it, she'd sworn off men, if not forever, at least for the next year. No distractions from her brand-new life plan. No complications. Definitely no time for a hot landlord.

Even more incentive for her to pretend sparks hadn't ignited when he'd touched her.

She turned away from him––maybe if she averted her gaze these butterflies beating in her belly would relax. "You've got my paperwork and check, right? Is there anything else you need? I'd like to get unpacked."

"Sure. Let me grab those other bags for you." He turned and sauntered toward the door.

She huffed out a breath. "No, that's fine. I can handle it."

"It's my pleasure. I insist," he called over one broad shoulder.

Was she being unreasonable? What was wrong with him being helpful? She sighed and pressed one hand over her aching heart.

"Here you go. I'll bring you the spare keys. Call if you need anything else." With one last heated look, Nick left the cottage.

Who would've known the universe could be so perverse? She'd come to Laguna Beach to heal her broken heart, to write her novel, and to focus on herself, not to hook up with a guy, no matter how hot he was. And Nicholas Morgan was mouthwateringly hot.

From now on, she planned on holing up in the cottage and writing. And walking on the beach. Alone. She'd simply not answer the door when he returned with the keys. Avoidance was an effective coping technique, right?

She sank into the fluffy evergreen cushions of her new couch and soaked up the phenomenal view. Her own personal vista. When Zack leaped into her lap, she stroked his silky fur and the tension slowly evaporated from her limbs.

If she couldn't heal her heart and start a new life in this quiet cottage, she couldn't do it anywhere.

Period.

SOPHIE'S VISION blurred as she stared at the computer screen. So much for her initial attempt at writing her book. Her stomach rumbled. *Groceries*––she needed groceries. She sprang up from her chair and snagged her purse.

She'd brave the rollercoaster ride into town and buy groceries. The stale protein bar she'd gnawed on this morning wasn't exactly the breakfast of champions. Once she'd stocked the kitchen with healthy food, she'd be calm and focused.

*Right.*

Somehow navigating down the twisting tree-lined lane was easier than her ascent. Amazing what a good night's sleep and a fresh environment could do. The Whole Foods was a quick drive down the Pacific Coast Highway. Charming restaurants and boutiques lined the main road through town, imparting a sense of sophistication. Hope for her fresh start filled her.

When she turned into the store's half-empty parking lot, she scored a spot close to the entrance. She grabbed a cart and cruised through the aisles. Grocery shopping soothed her—probably because she loved to eat so much. Not that she could cook, but she had serious vegetable-chopping skills and could scramble the heck out of an egg. Because she planned on chaining herself to her computer for the foreseeable future, she crammed the cart full of colorful produce, some staples, and enough chocolate to repair any crisis.

The checkout girl, tall and tan with a bouncy blond ponytail, smiled and asked if she was visiting town. Was Laguna so small that all the residents knew each other? What a concept.

Bemused, Sophie returned the smile and shared she'd just relocated from San Diego. When Blondie asked where she'd moved, Sophie's gut tightened. Her ex wouldn't come looking for her, certainly not at the grocery store.

She exhaled a steadying breath. "I rented a cute little cottage up the hill."

Blondie's eyes widened. "Oh, are you Nick's new tenant?"

"Um, yeah. How'd you guess?" She pulled out her wallet, schooling her expression. How tiny was this town?

"He and his sister are locals, and they put the word out they were looking for a reliable renter. So you must be reliable. Welcome to Laguna Beach." She stuck her hand across the register. "I'm Mallory, nice to meet you."

"Sophie." She could do this small-town gig.

"Are you single?"

Her mouth dropped open. Maybe she couldn't. "Excuse me?"

Mallory winked. "You know, single? Not dating? Looking for love?"

"Um, yes single, but not looking for love. Why?"

"Isn't Nick a hottie? You should totally go for it. Maybe you'll be the one that sticks." Mallory chattered as she bagged the groceries.

"The one that sticks?" What the what?

"Well, he's been single forever, and every woman in town wants him. Nobody lasts more than a few months. You should see his office manager chase after him—pretty obvious if you ask me. Not that I'm gossiping or anything. He and his buddy Brandt are heartbreakers."

Sophie's gut tightened. "Definitely not me. Thanks for the heads-up about him being a player, though. Good to know."

"Oh no, he's a nice guy. That came out wrong. He just never stays with one woman for very long, that's all." Mallory shrugged a shoulder.

"Thanks, I've got to run. Nice to meet you." She pasted on a smile.

Sophie hurried to her car, eager to return to her safe haven. She made it in record time and lugged the over-flowing bags into the house. The moment she placed the last shiny apple into the refrigerator, her cell phone rang.

Warmth filled her when she recognized her best friend's name on the screen. "Hey, what's up?"

"I'm calling to see how *you're* doing. I didn't hear from you last night and was worried," Kelly said.

"It was basically the trip from hell, but I finally made it to paradise. You wouldn't believe how peaceful the cottage is. I know I'll be able to write here. At some point, anyway." Niggling concerns over emptying half of her savings account and not having an actual income could be tossed into the vault for now.

"Oh, I'm so glad. Are you sure you won't come home? I miss you already."

Satisfaction filled her when she glanced around the cottage. It looked like hers now. Photos of her friends hanging out at the beach, one in front of the Eiffel Tower, and her favorite shot of the lighthouse in Kauai personalized the living room. A few novels waiting to be devoured lay on the coffee table, along with the latest issue of *Healthy Woman.*

"I miss you too, but this is my new home. I slept without interruption for the first time I can remember. You know what an insomniac I've been. I'm more certain about this move than anything I've done in the last four years."

"Relax and do nothing for a while. I'm envious that you'll be able to create your own schedule. Do you miss your insane hours at the magazine yet?"

Sophie snorted. "Yeah, no. I'm excited about my schedule too but it's a little nerve-wracking."

The beautiful day beckoned, and she stepped outside and crossed the verdant lawn. She sat down on the ornate wrought-iron bench and savored the salty air caressing her face and hair. She hummed with pleasure as the fragrant smell of flowers wafted into her nostrils.

"You've got a year to write your book. I know you need peace and quiet, but I worry about you isolating yourself. I'm coming to visit the first free weekend I have, okay?"

"I'd love that. Anything exciting happen since I left?" Time to change the subject.

Kelly cleared her throat. "Actually, yes. Part of the reason I called was because Doug showed up at my office today, demanding to know where you were. Claimed it was urgent he speak with you."

Her mouth went dry. "What? No, he can't find me. Why is he looking for me?" She dug her fingernails into her now sweaty palms.

"Don't worry. I told him to get lost. I'll never forgive the way that jerk treated you."

"Does he really think he can sweet talk me? This isn't about me. It's his Mr. Number One Salesman ego being unable to lose. I need to go. I'll call you soon." Sophie's phone slipped from her fingers onto the grass.

Unable to stop herself, she flashed back to the day, almost two months ago, when she'd been sipping champagne with her best friends as she prepared to walk down the aisle. She'd been cackling at one of her old friend's anecdotes from their high school misadventures when the wedding planner had knocked on the door of the hotel suite. Vanessa's complexion was chalky and her eyes damp when she handed her an envelope.

Doug's message had stopped her heart. He'd decided he didn't want to marry her.

She blinked furiously and dragged herself back to the present. No more blaming herself for trotting along, planning the wedding, without a clue he'd been sleeping with some bimbo for the previous eight months.

She would not shed another tear for him.

She'd pulled together the tattered remnants of her heart. Doug was a vampire who'd sucked out all her optimism, her light, and her strength. No man was ever getting that close to her again. Ever. The true love, marriage, family, and happily-ever-after life was for others, not for her.

She could have a fulfilling, wonderful life filled with meaningful work and her friends. A few no-strings hook-ups with guys sometime in the distant future would sustain her, thank you very much. She had Zack, who had adored her from the moment she rescued him. Animals' love was pure. They always loved you, no matter what.

It was enough.

It had to be enough.

Now she'd pour every ounce of passion she'd wasted on Doug into making her childhood dream of publishing a novel a reality. She'd only stayed at *Healthy Woman* so long because he'd demanded they had a double income to get married. Even when she'd fallen ill from the stressful deadline-driven position, he'd insisted she be practical.

Screw Doug.

And screw practical.

# CHAPTER 2

*N*ick guided his convertible BMW down the hill and drummed his fingers on the steering wheel. Sparks from the moment when he and Sophie's hands touched continued to reverberate through his system. What was it about her that immediately tugged at him? Sure, she was stunning, with her shiny mahogany hair, big sapphire eyes, and creamy skin.

But it wasn't simply physical. Was it her bubbly laughter when Bailey had leaped on her? She'd smelled delicious, like warm vanilla. Or maybe her obvious desire to get rid of him intrigued him?

Maybe he needed to get a life. Over the last few months, he had buried himself in drafting plans for the new art museum. Eager to create a unique masterpiece and leave his mark on the world forever with a building nobody would forget.

The sun warmed his skin as he cruised onto Highway 1 back to his office. Bailey sighed with joy in the passenger seat, the cool wind pressing her ears back. She'd stolen his heart the day he'd gone with a friend to the pound, with her liquid brown eyes beckoning to him from behind sterile metal bars. Although he loved living solo and being unencumbered, she'd reminded him of his beloved childhood mutt. Now he couldn't imagine life without her.

When he pulled into the office driveway, pride filled his chest at the Morgan Designs sign over the awning. Ever since he saw the soaring skyscrapers of Manhattan as a young boy, he'd never questioned his destiny. He'd decided then to follow in his architect father's footsteps and change the landscape, one building at a time.

He bounded up the stairs two at a time, eager to return to his comfort zone. Entering his office, he headed to his desk and Bailey plopped onto her dog bed. Before he could settle onto his stool, the phone rang.

"Have you met the new tenant yet?" his sister Alyssa demanded.

He ran his tongue around his teeth. "Yeah."

"And?"

"And, what?" No way would he admit his attraction to Sophie––especially not to his baby sister.

"What's she like? She's our first tenant since we decided to rent the cottage. I mean she applied and offered to pay for the whole year up front. Spill the details."

He rifled through the pile of papers on his desk for the museum plans. "Alyssa, I've got to get back to work."

"Did she like it? Is she old? Young? Pretty? Why did she move here so fast? Is she on the run?" His sister was famous for her tenacity.

All questions he wanted the answers to, but he needed to process his unprecedented primitive reaction to the woman first. Because what would he say? *Yeah, I'd wanted to rip off her clothes and toss her over my shoulder and carry her back to the bedroom...*

He frowned and exhaled a steadying breath. "She complimented your interior design skills, okay? Go meet her your-self. I've got to finish these plans this afternoon."

"Fine, I will."

Nick placed his phone on his desk and picked up his pencil. He had to review the timeline to complete his plans. But his curiosity was piqued. What secrets lurked behind Sophie's gorgeous eyes?

When he brought her a fresh set of keys, he looked forward to discovering some answers about the mysterious Ms. Sophie Barnes.

THE FOLLOWING AFTERNOON, Nick parked in front of the cottage. When he started toward the door, a muffled sound from the front yard caught his attention. He turned and there was Sophie on the garden bench. Switching gears, he crossed toward where she sat––her elbows on her knees, her dark head in her hands.

"Sophie?"

She shivered, massaged the skin on her bare arms, and lifted her head. Her face was pale, her eyes stormy and damp.

The raw emotion on Sophie's unguarded face twisted a knife in his own heart. He was no stranger to pain. "You okay?"

"You're stealing my sunlight." Her full pink lips turned down at the corners.

He stepped to the side and pulled the keys from his jeans pocket. "Better? I brought you the keys."

She rose and extended one artistic hand "Oh, well, thanks. I appreciate it."

Sparks flew again the moment her fingers brushed his. Every muscle in his body hardened. Her pupils flared, she snatched back her hand, and crossed her arms across her chest.

Yeah, she wasn't immune to him. "It's nothing. Bailey sends her apologies and insists I take you to dinner tomorrow night. There's a great Italian place at the bottom of the hill."

She smoothed a strand of silky hair behind her ear. "No, no thanks. I told you I love dogs so there's no need. I've got to get back to work."

"What work?" She'd definitely not been working.

She threw up both hands. "I write. I'm writing. Look, I'm sure you're a nice guy, but I have no interest in dating. I came here to simplify my life. So, if you don't mind, I really need to get back to it."

One question answered––she was a writer. And she had not been writing. She'd been upset about something.

"Come on, you'll love Marino's. It's casual and has the best pasta in Orange County. Look at it as a welcome to town dinner, not a date. I'll give you some tips about Laguna." His sister was not the only tenacious Morgan.

She narrowed her blue eyes at him. "Okay, fine, I'll go because I do have some questions about town and Italian is my favorite. But it's just dinner, nothing more. Understand?"

He pressed one hand against his chest. "Just dinner. Got it. I'll pick you up at seven." Dinner was a start... he'd never resorted to subterfuge to get a date before but something about Sophie stirred him despite her prickly behavior.

"Fine. I'll see you later." Sophie turned and marched toward the cottage.

Nick remained rooted to the spot, watching her until she slammed the front door. She looked adorable in snug yoga pants, with her mahogany hair in a messy ponytail. And damn did her sexy little body make a picture stalking away.

With a shake of his head, he turned and returned to his

car. Usually, he kept his relationships simple and commitment free. He enjoyed women, but if one began hinting at the white picket fence, he moved on to the next one. No ties. No problem. He didn't care if the small community of Laguna assumed he was a player.

Building his business over the last decade gave him all the satisfaction he required. No time existed for entanglements.

But he wanted to know why Sophie had moved to Laguna alone. Why she seemed so reluctant to go out with him when the chemistry between them crackled. He wasn't sure why he couldn't let it go, but until he got to know her, focusing on anything else was going to be tough. Tomorrow night couldn't come too soon.

## CHAPTER 3

*E*vaporated.
Vanished.

Talent, even talent that lay dormant and underutilized for years, still existed. It didn't just disappear, did it?

Computer up and running, check. Fresh glass of water with lemon, check. Comfortable clothes, meant to make it easy to sit at said computer for several hours uninterrupted, check. Zack curled up on her lap to lend moral support, check. Organized notes, ready to reference, check.

For the fiftieth time, she lifted her gaze to the window and soaked up the beautiful view. She wasn't procrastinating. She was just getting acclimated. Keep telling yourself that, lazy girl.

Why was this so much more challenging than writing an article for the magazine? Was she one of those people who just talked about writing? If only she had the time, she could pop out a novel, a witty tale of love and adventure?

For the first time in her adult life, endless hours dawned in front of her with no distractions, just time to write. No excuses. As a child, she'd written countless stories. They'd been so good she'd been published in a collection when she was twelve.

No longer the carefree confident girl who didn't worry about her audience, now she was paralyzed with journalistic training and relentless editing. And apparently she'd developed an innate talent for procrastination along the way.

Well, here went nothing.

She began to type.

When her alarm buzzed, she jolted. Looking at the timer on her phone, she realized she'd been writing for over three hours. Grinning like a loon, she jumped up and danced around the room. Maybe she could be a writer.

But creating the next hit novel would have to wait a little longer. For some reason, she'd agreed to dinner with Mr. Sex-on-a-Stick, and it was time to dive into the shower.

Thirty minutes later she glared at her closet. How could she have nothing to wear? She didn't have anyone to impress, so why couldn't she simply throw something on? It was a casual dinner, right? She rolled her eyes––the light gleaming in Nick's green eyes had been anything but casual. And she couldn't deny feeling the waves of chemistry sparking between them. What were the odds she chose celibacy and her landlord was the hottest guy she'd ever met?

Little black dress? Negative, too obvious, trying too hard. Sundress? No, too much skin. Her favorite high-necked top with black pants? Forget it, too businesslike. What could she wear that would scream she didn't want to date him but still feel attractive? What was wrong with her?

Thirty minutes in the closet was absurd. Imagine if she did want to impress him on their date? Oops, not date, "just dinner." Not having gone on a first date in more than four years, she no longer had a go-to, first-date ensemble. Or a go-to "just dinner" ensemble, for that matter.

She settled on her fallback outfit: a fitted V-neck black

top, paired with her favorite dark jeans and wedged sandals. She spent longer than she'd ever admit on her makeup, taking the time to play up her eyes. Just for herself, of course. *Keep telling yourself that, Sophie.*

When Nick arrived, she opened the door and that silly flutter appeared in her belly. Again. What was she Scarlett O'Hara now, fluttering at Rhett? And, really, what was fluttering?

He looked smoking hot, with his hair still damp and a casual black shirt tucked into dark jeans. Warmth bloomed in her cheeks, and she prayed her ivory skin didn't betray her.

He flashed a grin. "We match."

"Should I change?" Her lips twitched.

His heated gaze raked over her. "Definitely not. You're stunning. Ready?"

He opened the passenger door to his black BMW-- okay so he had manners. They zoomed down the hill toward the lights of Laguna proper, and she settled into the buttery-soft leather seat. Keeping her gaze on the scenery outside helped distract her from his magnetic presence.

And his hands. Those strong, masculine hands. When she'd first noticed them, she'd pictured them stroking along her skin. Large, square-palmed, and well-shaped. Golden hair glistened on his forearms, which rippled with sinewy muscle as he gripped the steering wheel.

Yes, she was in trouble. Big trouble. Focus on the scenery. Don't drool over his fascinating arms. Nothing like the smooth white hands of her ex, Doug. Time to distract herself from staring at his powerful hands.

"Is Marino's a regular haunt for you?" Dumb question. His presence seemed to relegate her intelligence to the back of the room.

"Yes, it's owned by old family friends. I love it. You'll see why."

Suddenly, a car screeched out in front of them. Nick slammed on the brakes, simultaneously reaching over to press her back against the seat.

Her nipples tightened, and goosebumps prickled on her skin. How could he elicit such a reaction with only the pressure of his arm? How annoying and unfair.

His gaze searched her face, concern etched in his chiseled features. "Crazy drivers. Are you okay, Sophie?"

She smoothed a strand of hair away from her face. "I'm fine. No worries."

He glanced at her with a raised brow. "Cold?"

"No, I'm fine. Just a little startled." More like turned on.

*Get a grip.* She wiped her sweaty palms on her jeans and looked out the window. Time to stop acting like a naïve schoolgirl at the sight of the latest Hollywood heartthrob.

"We made it." He pulled up to the entrance of a beautiful terra-cotta building with large windows and a slanted roof. Subtle cursive lettering above the doorway spelled Marino's.

At least she wouldn't be confined in the small car with him anymore. "It looks like we're going to someone's house."

His lips curved upward. "No, they just like it secluded and cozy."

"Buona sera, signorina." A valet was instantly at her door, offering a welcoming hand as she stepped out of the car.

"Grazie," she replied, using one of her token Italian words.

"Welcome, Nicholas. Welcome. Isabella has your table waiting for you. Quick, quick, go inside so your lady doesn't catch a chill."

Nick rested one hand lightly on her lower back and escorted her through the ornate carved wooden door into a charming, candlelit lobby. Deep rose-colored walls imparted warmth. Subtle music played in the background, and white-clothed tables filled the two rooms adjoining the lobby area.

A stunning brunette with a wide smile and outstretched hands approached them.

"Nicholas, it's been too long since you've joined us. Where have you been hiding?" Her gaze flicked toward Sophie.

He shrugged a broad shoulder. "I'm just working a lot, Isabella. This is Sophie."

"Of course. Welcome, Sophie. Follow me."

Isabella led them to a cozy table tucked in the corner, against an enormous window. Delicious aromas filled the air. Every cell in her body was on high alert, Nick's proximity tempting her to lean back into his palm. What was going on with her?

An open bottle of wine and two glasses sat on the table.

"I think someone is already sitting here," Sophie said.

"No, I requested the bottle be opened so it had plenty of time to breathe. I hope you don't mind I took the liberty of selecting the wine." He pulled out her chair, his hands brushing against her shoulder. The hairs on the back of her neck prickled.

He was definitely smooth. She'd noticed his confidence at her house, but not the polished veneer. Sophie hated to admit it, but she loved when a man took charge in certain situations. She wasn't about to divulge her secret, though. Imagine what he would do with that information.

"I'm sure it'll be fine. I love wine, so you really can't go wrong in that arena."

Before he could reply, an elegantly clad silver-haired man arrived at their table.

"Nicholas, welcome. Are you going to have the usual tonight, or can I bring you and your lady some menus?" The waiter lilted in his lovely Italian accent.

Nick arched his brow at her. "I usually take the special here. Alberto is an amazing chef. Are you game, or would you like to order off the menu?"

"I am sure whatever Alberto prepares will be wonderful." She beamed at the waiter.

The waiter nodded with a smile and hurried away.

"How often do you come here?" Did he bring all his dates here? A new one every night?

He shrugged a shoulder and lifted the bottle. "It's my favorite restaurant. Wine?"

"Please. California wine instead of Italian? Is that allowed?" Her lips twitched.

He laughed. "Funny. They don't care. This is one of my favorite zinfandels from Sonoma."

When he filled her glass, his fingers brushed hers again. Heat shot straight to her center and her heart thrummed in her chest. She drew her hand back and resolved to keep her mind above the table.

Flings were in her future, just not yet. One problem. Her body wasn't quite cooperating with her mind.

He shifted back in his seat. "So what brought you to Laguna from San Diego?"

She stiffened, refusing to allow memories of Doug to ruin her appetite. "It's a long story, and I don't want to bore you with the details."

"You couldn't bore me." He reached across the table and squeezed her hand.

She jolted and once again her nipples pebbled. She downed half her glass of wine before responding.

"I was an editor at *Healthy Woman*. I'd been planning on taking a sabbatical, but I realized I never wanted to go back, so I guess I quit my job."

"I've seen that magazine. What happened?" Nick leaned closer and his clean beachy scent reached her nostrils.

"The job was fine…" She polished off the rest of her wine. At this rate, she'd be buzzed by the time the entrees arrived. *Slow down, Sophie.*

"Being an editor was extremely stressful, and then some things, um, some things shifted. My dream was always to be a writer. Who knows, I could bomb out with this, but I had to try. What is it they say? It's better to regret the things you've done instead of those you haven't?" She shrugged, setting down the empty glass.

"I think that's great you're following your dreams. Carpe diem, right?" He refilled her glass before toasting her.

She gestured with her wine. "Seizing the day, that's me."

Nick quirked a brow. "But why now? Most people aren't brave enough to jump without a net."

"Come on, trading in wearing grown-up clothes at the office to writing in my pajamas with my cat on my lap? Who could resist?" She winked. "Tell me what you do besides rent cottages?"

"Sure. I'm an architect."

"So you've read *The Fountainhead*, right? Are you following in Roark's footsteps?" Howard Roark was one of her favorite literary heroes.

"It's my favorite book. I hope to make my mark…" For the first time, a flicker of uncertainty clouded his gaze.

Architects were trailblazers, creative visionaries––it helped give her a clearer image of who he was. Her shoulders softened. "To fulfilling dreams. Tell me more."

He shared fascinating stories about his favorite buildings around the country and his latest projects. Light conversation and laughter dominated the rest of the meal. Nick was easy to talk to and could keep up with her lightning quick changes of topics. How refreshing was that?

And a major contrast to Doug, who used to snap at her to focus on one thing at a time. Jerk.

～

NICK POURED the last of the wine. He smiled at her across the table, his gorgeous eyes crinkling at the corners. Any last vestiges of doubt about joining him for dinner disappeared and she returned his smile.

Without warning, he leaned across the table, cupped her face in his hands, and brushed her mouth with his. Gentle, at first. Unable to resist, her lips parted, and she swirled her tongue against his. He tasted like her favorite wine mixed with something uniquely his own. Delicious. Heat bloomed low in her belly.

With a growl, he deepened the kiss, threading his fingers into her hair and pulling her closer.

"Let's get out of here, sweetheart. Let's go back to my place," he murmured against her lips.

She jerked back as if he'd slapped her. Her pulse hammered in her throat and her spine stiffened.

Fury replaced her complacency. "I knew it! Welcome to the neighborhood, my ass. You took advantage. This 'casual dinner' is finished."

He held up both hands. "Sophie. Sophie, calm down. It was just a kiss. I just—"

"I don't want to hear it. Now take me home, or I'm getting an Uber." She pushed away from the table.

"Hold on. Please sit down."

She sank back into her seat––not wanting to make a scene. "Fine. I just want to go home. Alone."

"Let me settle the check, and we'll go. Seriously, Sophie, I misread your signals and was out of line. I'm sorry." He rubbed one hand along the back of his neck.

"Fine." She clasped her hands in her lap and maintained her distance while he paid the bill, and they exited the restaurant.

So much for a casual dinner. She'd be avoiding her land-lord from now on. Tonight had been a mistake. Just like she knew it would be. So much for trusting her intuition.

Silence weighed heavy on the ride back to the cottage. When he attempted to speak to her, she held up her hand. "No."

He focused on the road for the remainder of what now seemed like an interminable distance. The car pulled up to her doorway, where she exited without a word or a back-ward glance.

She commended herself for not slamming the door.

# CHAPTER 4

*N*ick raked his fingers through his hair, tossed his pencil down on his architect's desk, and stalked to the window. How had last night gone so wrong? Maybe he'd pressured Sophie into having dinner, but he hadn't imagined the flare of attraction in her big sapphire eyes when they'd met.

From the moment he'd picked her up last night, his awareness had deepened. From the quick stop on the drive down when he'd reached out to protect her and her tight nipples had drilled into his arm. Hell, he'd almost pulled over right then and kissed her. Then during dinner she'd let her guard down, and her wit and her easy laughter mesmerized him. He couldn't remember when he'd laughed so much on a date.

He admired her choice to go for her dreams and take risks. Her genuine interest in architecture and his ambitions had warmed him. Her inner beauty shone through her external appeal, and he'd been unable to resist the impulse to kiss her.

*Idiot.* Because he'd obviously misinterpreted her signals––

she'd been livid after he kissed her. Although her plump parted lips, wide eyes, and flushed cheeks seemed to signal anger wasn't her initial reaction.

He stared out at the brilliant blue sky––until he figured out what to do about her, drafting the new wing of the Memorial Hospital wasn't going to happen.

"Knock, knock, anyone there?"

He turned and Alyssa stood framed in the doorway. His stunning younger sister was tall, lean, and built like a gazelle. Just like their mother. He loved Alyssa more than anyone on earth and respected her opinions. Maybe she could help him figure it out?

She crossed her arms across her chest. "Why the long face? You look like you're trying to unlock the solution to world peace or something. What's going on?"

"Sorry, just running through some numbers on the latest project. Nothing serious." *Liar.*

"Well, I just had lunch at Marino's and heard some fascinating news…Isabella mentioned you had a romantic date last night. Who's the flavor of the week?"

"I don't have flavors of the week." He pointed at her. "You know I'm not like that."

Accustomed to her busting his balls, he usually took her teasing in stride. Because she was his only living relative, his devotion necessitated he tolerate her sarcasm and her seemingly boundless capacity to give him crap.

This time, he swallowed his customary acerbic reply. Sophie was different. Perhaps his sister could go over and assess the situation. Maybe she could shed some light on the mystery that was Sophie Barnes. Because he'd sure as hell never had to pursue a woman before.

"Hmmm…Anyway, rumor is you staked out a secluded table in the corner, with a special vintage decanting prior to arriving. Not your usual MO. And something about a sultry little brunette?" Her enormous eyes glowed with mischief.

Nick cursed his sister's tenacity and kept his expression impassive. She'd been trying to marry him off for the last few years. If his younger sister suspected he was hooked on Sophie, he'd never hear the end of it.

"Isabella needs to mind her own business. It was just a casual dinner."

"If it was so casual, why aren't you telling me who it is? That new girl at Steve's office? A little surf bunny from the beach?" Alyssa wrinkled her nose. "Just please don't tell me you took Heather to dinner. Anyone but her."

"Heather's in her office. Stop."

His office manager, Heather, was an attractive brunette with a Harvard MBA and killer instincts. She worked her ass off, and in the last year, her connections played an instrumental role in setting him up as a contender for architecture's coveted Pritzker Prize. He couldn't afford to piss her off. For the last fifteen years, his sole focus, besides raising his baby sister, was to become one of the top architects in the country, just like his father.

"Look, you can bury your head in the sand all you want, but it's clear she wants to jump your bones. That woman looks at you like you're a forbidden devil's food cupcake, and she's on day five of a juice cleanse."

"You missed your calling in Hollywood. No more drama, please? Heather's help creating my submission package and her ties to the Pritzker committee are huge. You know I've been passed over for the last few years, and she's making a difference for me. Can we drop it?"

Alyssa's disdain for Heather was out of character. She was usually compassionate and rarely judgmental. But she insisted Heather seemed sneaky and fake. He didn't see it.

Her face softened immediately. She hurried over and

hugged him. "I know the Pritzker is your tribute to Dad, but it won't bring him back. It doesn't change all you've already accomplished. You know that, right?"

He turned back toward his desk and massaged the iron cords on the back of his neck. Their parents had died in a car crash when he was nineteen and Alyssa was fourteen, altering their lives forever. He'd raised his younger sister on his own while finishing college. Building his business with the intent to honor his late father's legacy required he keep his relationships simple and commitment free. How he liked it.

"Fine." She raised her dark blonde brows. "So who was it?"

Damn, she was relentless. He blew out a breath.

"Okay, okay, I took the new tenant to dinner." He glanced back and groaned at her smug expression.

She pressed one hand to her throat. "Wow, sweet of you. Was that part of the rental agreement? Hmmm… So how did it go?"

"It was just dinner." He frowned. Of course it wasn't just dinner. His sleepless night proved that. Two cold showers failed to cool down his teenager-like hormones.

"Sure." She rolled her eyes. "Does that mean it wasn't really a date and you weren't trying to impress her? Are you going to see her again?"

"Stop with the twenty questions, okay? No plans. She does seem alone. Maybe you should drop by and welcome her to the neighborhood."

He gritted his teeth. Why hadn't he thought his brilliant idea through? Because painting Sophie as lonely and having Alyssa befriend her wouldn't exactly help his cause. *Damn it.*

Alyssa waggled her eyebrows. "Great idea. You know I'm curious about her. Shall I ask her about your date?"

He grimaced. "It wasn't a date. And don't ask her about it either." And now they'd reverted to grade school.

"Calm down, dear brother, calm down. Methinks thou doth protest too much." With a quick wave, she exited as quickly as she'd appeared.

He heard a click and hoped it was Alyssa letting herself out and not Heather next door. No need to antagonize his right-hand person.

Now that his sister was going to check on Sophie, his shoulders softened.

With a resolute sigh, he faced his desk, picked up his pencil, and shoved his feelings into the vault.

SOPHIE SPLASHED cold water on her pale face in a vain attempt to shock some color into her ghost-like demeanor. The sleepless night showed. Not that she was planning on entertaining visitors today, but nobody enjoyed resembling death warmed over. Good thing Zack approved of her no matter what she looked like.

Damn Nicholas Morgan. He was the sole snag in her simple new life. An unwelcome complication. Well, she'd start today fresh and relegate last night to the past, where it belonged. He was her landlord, nothing more, nothing less.

With ruthless precision, she checked her calendar and grinned because all she had scheduled today was to write. All day if she felt like it. At least for one thousand words if she didn't.

New day.

New opportunity.

She placed a steaming mug of her favorite spearmint green tea on the coaster next to the computer. She piled sliced bananas, strawberries, juicy raspberries, and vanilla wafers on a cheerful yellow plate for nibbling. Her favorite grapefruit candle offered its fragrant bouquet. No reason for her to be distracted or leave her computer for the foreseeable future.

After a few false starts, she dug in and committed to writing without stopping. Everyone advised her to sit down and let it flow, without worrying about the language, the prettiness of the prose, even whether it made any sense. She considered herself a true student of the Hemingway school of writing, where you wrestled the words until you'd found only the perfect ones and jettisoned the rest. Her journalism training didn't help either.

And, big shocker, until her doorbell rang, her fingers flew across her keyboard. Stretching like a cat, she rose and strolled toward the door. Her breath caught and she halted in the middle of the room. What if it was Nick?

Donning an imaginary suit of armor to combat his charm, just in case, she approached the door. A sharp knock alerted her she was taking her sweet time. The additional prodding only served to stiffen her resolve to be cool and collected if it was her tempting landlord. When she opened the door, she blinked at the stunning blond holding a cellophane-wrapped plate of cookies. Wow, were supermodels delivering cookies these days?

"Hi, I'm Alyssa, Nick's sister." The tall willowy goddess-like creature, with bouncy Victoria's Secret waves smiled, revealing perfect white teeth. "I brought you some of my famous oatmeal cookies."

"Hi, thanks so much. I'm Sophie. I'll put on some tea. You need to help me eat these." As if she needed more sugar after she'd reduced the box of wafers to a few measly crumbs. At this rate, her blood sugar levels would explode.

Alyssa didn't bat an eyelash at Sophie's sweats, messy

topknot, and wan complexion. "I'd love to. I hope I'm not interrupting anything…"

"Oh no, I've been writing, and I could use a break. Come on in. The kitchen is right through here." She laughed. "Oh yeah, you lived here, so you would know that."

They strolled back to the kitchen and Alyssa placed the cookies on the granite counter and Sophie filled the kettle. While the tea brewed, they chatted about the weather and all those trivial things that made it easier to feel comfortable in a small room with a total stranger.

Returning to the living room, they settled onto the comfy couch. Sophie sampled a cookie and her eyes fluttered shut and she moaned. Alyssa wasn't kidding about the cookies being fame worthy. "Oh my god, these are amazing."

Alyssa's lips twitched. "I'm glad you like them. So you're a writer? What are you working on?"

"My first novel. I quit my job and figured isolating myself would really help me focus on writing. You know, new place, no friends, no distractions." Although the Morgan siblings weren't helping with their impromptu visits.

"Except for me dropping in unannounced. Sorry about that. But that's amazing. You're braver than me. Were you scared to walk away from the security of a regular paycheck?"

"No, seriously, I needed a break and I appreciate you stopping by." She pressed a hand to Alyssa's slender arm. "To tell you the truth, my mom, my ex-boss, and most of my friends think I've lost my mind. I was on track to be promoted to managing editor for *Healthy Woman* magazine, but I felt trapped. Like if I took that position, I'd work sixty hours forever and never write my novel."

Why was it so easy to express herself to Alyssa when she'd found it challenging to explain her fears to people who'd known her for years? Doug had always mocked her secret ambitions, never understanding her creative drive.

Alyssa tilted her head. "I think that's wonderful. What do they say? You only regret the things you don't try? What's it about?"

"Funny, I just said that last night... Anyway, without going into detail, the book is about love, loss, and redemption. But I'm not ready to share details, sorry." She sipped her tea and contemplated a second cookie.

Alyssa waved a hand. "No worries. I get it. Some people love to share, and others keep it close to their heart. So have you had a chance to explore Laguna yet?"

"Not really. My priority is writing, although I'd love any Vinyasa yoga studio recommendations. With my new cookie habit, I really need to balance out my days with some physical activity."

"I love yoga. I go to a great studio called Om Yoga. Why don't you come with me tomorrow morning? My favorite teacher's class starts at nine. And maybe we could grab breakfast afterward?"

Happiness filled her. "Sure, I'd love to. Thanks so much for offering."

"Thanks so much for taking a few moments to hang out. I know it can be tough to start fresh somewhere new." Alyssa set down her cup and stood. "Did Nick make sure you have everything you need?"

Sophie pressed one hand to her belly. "Uh...yeah...sure. I'm good."

Considering Nick and "need" in the same sentence would send her down a dangerous path. Last night had been a sleepless one, punctuated by memories of his firm lips on hers. Imagining what his tanned skin looked like below the open collar of his shirt. Fantasizing about if the rest of his body was as hard and sinewy as his muscular forearms.

Alyssa's eyes widened, and Sophie prayed she hadn't caught her hesitation. She needed a friend a lot more than she needed to get involved with any man. Because she planned to employ some self-discipline and avoid him at all costs.

No more smooth-talking, fast-moving gorgeous players for her.

No distractions.

CHAPTER 5

After an hour of vigorous Vinyasa yoga, Sophie melted into her mat, every cell in her body warm and soft. Sometimes turning off her overactive brain was tough, but today she'd found blessed relaxation during Savasana, yoga's final resting pose.

Bliss.

When the teacher invited them to return to a seated position, contentment filled her. Daily yoga practice was her new life's missing puzzle piece. Life suddenly seemed simple. She rolled up her green yoga mat, grabbed her aluminum water bottle, and smiled over at Alyssa.

"You were so right. This was fantastic. Exactly what I needed."

Alyssa's smile was serene. "Yes, she's inspiring, right? I love her class, and the other instructors here are great too."

Together, they headed to brunch. Strolling down the quaint cobblestone sidewalk off the main drag in Laguna, Sophie drank in the scenery.

"Wow, Laguna is so charming. I can't believe how

different it feels from San Diego. It even smells different. More fragrant somehow."

Alyssa nodded. "I agree. San Diego is gorgeous, but there's something special about this little stretch of coast. It reminds me of the Riviera. Have you ever been?"

"I have. My mom's from Agen, a small town in the South of France. We used to travel there when I was a kid and visited Nice and Antibes. I love it." Sophie's stomach growled. "Are we close?"

"We're here. My favorite little French bistro." Alyssa waved toward a patio with brightly colored mosaic-tiled tables and cane-woven chairs, all enclosed by a black wrought iron fence. "Let's sit outside. The food's delicious, and the coffee is to die for."

They chose a table located under a giant eucalyptus tree that cloaked them in a hint of dappled sunlight and partial shade. A waitress in a black skirt and crisp white shirt approached and handed them two menus. They ordered café au lait and perused the brunch options.

Sophie's tummy grumbled again, eager for a meal someone else had prepared. Eating at home made the most sense now she didn't have a regular paycheck. Oh yeah, and because she wasn't a fan of dining out solo.

When the waitress returned with their coffees, they both ordered croissants with spinach-and-cheddar-cheese omelets. Alyssa shared her passion for artistic expression and how it impacted her interior-design career. No wonder the cottage was so cozy and welcoming.

While they ate, Alyssa's phone beeped. With an apologetic glance, she picked up the call.

"Hey, Nick, what's up? Oh, shoot, no, I totally forgot you were headed to New York today. You want to drop Bailey off now? I've got to head to L.A. this afternoon and totally spaced about keeping her for you." She frowned.

Sophie was laser focused on Alyssa's responses. What was wrong with her? She heard Nick's name, and her pulse kicked up—his potent presence even affected her through the phone. And she wasn't even on the phone with him. *Pathetic.*

"I'm so sorry, but I can't. Why can't Brandt take her? Hmmm, what about doggy daycare? I could swing by and drop her off for you."

Alyssa huffed out a breath, then her gaze flicked toward Sophie and her eyes widened. "Hold on. I may have a solution."

*Uh-oh.*

"I hate to ask, but is there any way you could watch Bailey for the next few days? I need to go to L.A. for business. Please? Bailey knows the cottage, and she's such a sweet girl. It would be a huge help. I could pay you for the time..."

Alyssa was a velvet hammer. Or a bulldozer. How could she refuse without being rude? It wasn't like she had anywhere to be except the cottage. And if Bailey were Alyssa's dog, she wouldn't hesitate to pet-sit.

Damn, damn, damn, this meant she'd have to see Nick again. Because that wouldn't be awkward after the other night. Because she hadn't been able to forget about their mind-blowing kiss.

No temptation needed, thank you very much. "Sure, of course. A couple of days. Will you bring her over?"

Alyssa held up one perfectly manicured finger and spoke to Nick. "I've got the perfect solution. Sophie agreed to keep Bailey at the cottage, isn't that sweet? We're just finishing up breakfast, and then we can swing by and pick her up."

Alyssa nodded. "Okay, if time's that tight, I'll drop Sophie off and you bring Bailey straight to the cottage. Twenty minutes, okay? Bye."

Alyssa's smile was sheepish. "I owe you big time. Let's

finish up, and I'll take you home. He's heading out, and it's easier for him to drop Bailey off."

Sophie savored the kiss of the warm breeze through her hair while they cruised up the hill in Alyssa's white convertible Beemer. She could handle seeing Nick again, despite the tell-tale nerves flickering in her belly. She willed her system to quiet as she absorbed the beautiful tree-lined street leading up to her new home. Her home.

Satisfaction filled her––she was independent, going to yoga, making a new friend, and writing her book. All the things she'd sacrificed while struggling to succeed at her hectic job and please Doug.

Having a temporary dog playmate would be great. It was irrelevant that Bailey belonged to Nick, right? As a child, she'd yearned for a pet, but her mother disliked any kind of hairy beast. Then, Doug hated dogs. Why had she allowed him to control so many aspects of her life?

Taking Bailey for walks would be a great way to explore the neighborhood. It wasn't like Zack would submit to a leash. He preferred to run and play on his own schedule. Usually at around five in the morning, when he'd walk all over her pillow to wake her for his breakfast.

When they pulled into the driveway, Nick was leaning against his car. In tailored slate-colored slacks and a crisp white dress shirt highlighting his broad shoulders, flat abs, and narrow hips, he was gorgeous. Heat curled down her spine.

She'd barely shut the car door when Alyssa waved goodbye, revved into reverse, and sped down the driveway. Odd. Alyssa hadn't mentioned being in a hurry.

Bemused, she waved and braced herself to face Nick. Bailey bounded over, slapped two enormous paws on her shoulders, and lathered her face with kisses. Déjà vu.

She laughed, thankful for the dog playing intermediary.

"Hi, so do you have her things together for me? Any special instructions?"

"Her stuff is on the porch. Sorry about my sister. She's usually not forgetful, so thanks." He shook his head. "But I'm warning you. Bailey will try to climb in bed and cuddle with you under the sheets."

Heat rose in her cheeks, and she cursed her fair skin. Now the visual of his rangy, muscular body pressing her back into the sheets filled her already over-active imagination. Those powerful hands roaming all over her. His mouth. On every single inch of her body.

They needed to change the subject.

Pronto.

No more talk of cuddling under her bed's sheets.

She swallowed, seeking relief for her now-arid throat. "Nice. I'm sure she and Zack will battle for the best spot. Lucky for me, it's a king bed."

His jaw tightened before he turned and picked up the dog's supplies. *Crap.* Was he coming inside with her? Despite her post-yoga contentment, Sophie's entire system zipped and zapped and went haywire. When she opened the front door, he held it while she and Bailey entered the house. Her breasts brushed against his chest and arm and the heat he emanated flamed through her. She sucked in a fortifying breath, her senses clouding when his clean masculine scent filled her nostrils.

"I thought you had a plane to catch? Don't you need to leave?" Oops, that was rude. Whatever. She was still angry with him. Wasn't she?

"Sophie." Nick's voice was raspy.

She turned and he placed his hands on her shoulders, his long fingers scorching her through her thin jacket. Her nipples were hard enough to cut glass, and a spear of heat shot straight down to her center.

His emerald eyes blazed. "Are you still mad at me?"

Sophie dropped her gaze and wrestled with the overwhelming urge to climb him like a tree. "I'm not mad. I'm just––hmmm…" *Dying for you to kiss me again and see if our chemistry is really that explosive.*

The urge to pounce on him grew overwhelming. Maybe she was just sexually deprived. Or hadn't she read about born-again virgin syndrome? She hadn't slept with another man in over four years. Yes, that must be it.

Maybe she just needed to jump Nick's bones and be done with it.

No strings.

No emotional attachment.

Just burning up those wonderful eight-hundred-count sheets.

Why was she fighting this? She was twenty-eight years old, a big girl. Having a fling might be the perfect solution to getting over Doug once and for all. Wipe the slate clean. Right now, she couldn't find a single reason not to pounce on him.

Something inside her snapped.

Sophie reached up and wound her arms around his neck, plastering her body against his. Nick's eyes widened a split second before she tugged his head down and kissed him, nipping his lower lip.

After a moment imitating a statue, Nick slanted his mouth across hers, deepening the kiss. His chest rumbled and his arms closed like iron bands around her. One hand slid down to her bottom and dragged her against his muscular frame. Every rock-hard inch of him.

Nick ripped his mouth away, nibbled down the side of her neck, and goosebumps erupted along her skin. When he brushed his parted lips across her collarbone, her head dropped back. He threaded one hand into her hair, holding her in place, and captured her mouth again. She melted against his hot hard body.

Bailey barked in excitement and jumped up to join in the game. They broke apart Eyes wide and wild, they stared at each other. Sophie struggled to catch her breath. Time to rein in whatever *that* had been. Because she'd been ready to tear off his clothes and have her way with him on the living room rug.

Nick grinned. "So does that mean you aren't mad at me, after all?"

Sophie struggled to slow her hammering heartbeat. What had gotten into her? She'd read about irrepressible passion in the steamy romance novels she loved to devour but assumed it was simply fiction.

Until now.

Until Nick.

"Umm, I don't, I don't…" She released a shaky exhale. "Wow."

She ran her fingers through her now really messed-up hair and turned toward the living room window.

"Sophie, I hate to do this, but I have a plane to catch. Spend Friday night with me?" Nick's crooked smile was devastating.

She retreated a step and attempted to ignore the sparks dancing along her skin. "No, I'm sorry I can't. My friend Kelly's coming to visit from San Diego."

A line appeared between his brows. "Sophie…"

She clasped her hands together, squeezing them tight, safe from his lethal touch. "Now it's my turn to apologize for kissing you. I don't know what got into me, but it can't happen again. I'm sorry but I can't have any complications in my life right now."

Because hopping into bed with him would be a mistake, chemistry or not. Her resolution not to get involved with

41

anyone for a year was the right thing to do. The sensible path. Maybe after a cold shower or ten, she'd be able to rekindle her dedication to living like a nun.

"I don't have time to debate, but we will see each other when I get back. And not just for me to pick up Bailey." Nick lifted her hand to his lips and placed a searing kiss in the middle of her palm. "Sweet dreams, beautiful. Don't miss me too much."

With a wink, he disappeared out the door.

# CHAPTER 6

*S*ophie woke with a start. She kicked her legs to untangle the sheets entwined around her sweaty legs. Blinking the sleep away, she reached toward the other side of the bed, her fingers hitting lush fur.

Zack and Bailey were snuggled together. Yeah––her landlord's dog. Not her hot landlord.

A dream.

Just a dream.

Time to hit replay. Nick had her pinned against the shower wall, buried to the hilt, her legs wrapped around his waist and his teeth grazing her neck. Steamy water coursed over them. No wonder she was burning up. Their passionate lovemaking had seemed so real.

Shaking off the dream and her sheets, she rose and headed to the kitchen to brew coffee. Before she sat down to write, she'd mainline caffeine and walk Bailey. Or as the older gentleman pruning his bougainvillea yesterday had called out, "Miss, who's walking who?" She'd laughed because clearly, Bailey was in charge.

Only problem: having Nick's dog around caused her to fixate on him more.

Time to escape from her obsessive thoughts about Nick and spin that energy into her book's hero. Maybe she could use her racy dream as inspiration for a spicy scene.

SOPHIE'S PHONE BUZZED––A text from Kelly alerting her she was almost to the cottage. She ran out the door and greeted her friend after she parked her cute cherry red hatchback.

Kelly wrapped her into a bear hug. "You weren't exaggerating how beautiful it is here."

"Isn't it? Just like you. I'm so happy you're here." She stepped back and admired her best friend's long beachy waves and unusual caramel-colored eyes.

Sophie grabbed Kelly's hand. "Come see my awesome new place."

Before they could cross the yard, Bailey rushed out, jumped up, and started licking Kelly's face.

"Bailey, Bailey, get down." Nick's giant mutt plopped her butt down and grinned up at them.

"Umm...when did you get a dog?" Kelly's eyes widened.

Sophie ran her tongue around her teeth. "Oh, I am just watching her for...um...for a friend. I mean for my landlord."

Kelly's gaze sharpened. "Really?"

"No big deal. My landlord's sister, Alyssa, who is great by the way, was supposed to watch her, but they crossed wires. It's not a big deal." She shrugged and reached for Kelly's tote bag.

"Okay. Well, Bailey seems like fun." Kelly's brow creased. "Anyway, I've been worried. You look tired."

She smoothed back her ponytail. "Thanks so much. Just

what I wanted to hear. I haven't been sleeping well. Let's go inside and catch up over tea."

Kelly shook her head. "Tea? I don't want tea. It's wine time."

"Sure. It's five o'clock somewhere, right? I've got your favorite pinot grigio in the fridge. Does that work?" She'd missed her best friend.

Kelly checked out the cottage on the way to the kitchen. "Definitely. This place is great. How's the writing going?"

"I just spent the last two hours and, oh, let's call it, forty-two minutes and thirty-six seconds writing. Once I force myself to sit and write, it flows. It's different than writing magazine articles. But I think I love this. I hope so. Geez, I'm rambling, aren't I?" She uncorked the wine and grabbed two glasses.

Kelly gave her a one-arm hug. "No, I love to hear you so passionate."

They meandered into the living room and settled onto the couch and Sophie tucked her legs up underneath her. Immediately, Zack jumped up to snuggle with them. Bailey flopped down on the rug, eager to join the party.

Kelly poured the wine and handed her a glass. "So why do you look so wiped out? Are you still losing sleep over Doug?"

"No, he hasn't been on my mind. Less and less each day." She shook her head.

Was that the understatement of the century? No need to share her preoccupation with sleeping with her landlord. Kelly knew her too well, and she wasn't ready to analyze her mixed feelings for Nick.

"Okay, and you're sure you want to stay? I'm sure you could get your job back and at least have financial security."

Sophie waved a hand. "No way. You know that job almost drove me to a nervous breakdown. I've got my savings. I need to go after my dream. Doug's betrayal was just the universal boot. I love my cottage and I know I can write this novel." Not having a regular paycheck didn't bother her one bit. Mostly.

Kelly patted Sophie's leg. "I'm sorry to be such a worry-wart—you've been through so much with your family and now Doug. You're one of the strongest, bravest people I know, but you've had a rough few months."

"Thanks, I love you. But let's focus on this weekend. We'll have a great time. Alyssa recommended a few restaurants and there are tons of art galleries here."

Kelly's tawny eyes widened. "You haven't even been out to a restaurant yet?"

"A couple of times." Sophie bit her lip. No need to bring up "the kiss" at Marino's. "And we'll see more together. So what's going on with you?"

Kelly's expression darkened. "Well, I was going to wait to bring this up, but we may as well get it out of the way. It's about Doug."

"Oh, screw him. I don't want to give him any more airtime, he doesn't deserve it." She slammed her wineglass onto the table, splashing the golden liquid.

"I think you need to hear this, just so you're prepared."

"Okay." Why the hell couldn't Doug just slither back under some rock, where he belonged? Hadn't he done enough damage?

"Remember when I told you he was asking about where you were and saying he had to speak with you?"

Sophie nodded, wiping her now-damp palms on her yoga pants.

"So Elizabeth told me he went by the magazine last week and demanded your address, claiming it was urgent he reach you. That he'd contacted your mom who refused to speak to him. He tried to pull this contrite, humble facade like he wanted to apologize. She wouldn't give it to him, but it concerns me. You're isolated up here. What if he shows up on your doorstep?"

Sophie surged to her feet and paced around the living room. "First of all, why does he want to see me? He stood me up at the damn altar. He cheated on me for months. He humiliated me. I never want to see his lying face again."

"I'm worried. He's always been a control freak and seems to be going nuts knowing you're gone. Do you want me to call and threaten him with a restraining order? I'm happy to do it." Her maid of honor for the ill-fated wedding gestured with her wineglass. "In fact, I'd love to do it."

Sophie inhaled a steadying breath and returned to the couch. She took a long drink of the pale straw-colored wine, savoring the crisp flavor, trying to cleanse the bad taste the thought of her ex literally put in her mouth.

"No, forget him. You know I couldn't get a restraining order at this point anyway. I can't imagine he'd get violent. No more Doug discussion. Tell me what's going on with you. How's Robert?"

Kelly's golden complexion paled. "Well, actually, nothing is going on with him."

"Nothing?"

"Things are weird right now between us. Let's just pretend those San Diego men don't exist, okay?" Kelly reached for the wine and refilled their glasses.

Fine with her.

Kelly updated Sophie on her job at her father's law firm and their mutual friends in San Diego. "Oh, and Elizabeth mentioned she'd hire you back in a heartbeat."

"Of course, my ex-boss wants me back. I did my job and hers for too many years." No way would she return to the corporate grind.

Nor would she allow people to take advantage of her any longer.

"I hear you. My career needs a change too—I wish I could do something creative like you." Kelly shrugged a shoulder. "Oh well, someone has to be the boring one."

Sophie rolled her eyes. "Yeah, boring is not a word anyone would ever apply to you."

A loud knock sounded at the door. Zack meowed and leaped gracefully off the couch with a barking Bailey hot on his heels. They raced to the front door.

Kelly pressed one hand against her throat. "Oh my god, you don't think it's Doug do you?"

"Don't be silly. We're just getting worked up about nothing," Sophie swallowed.

Forcing herself not to run, she rose, strolled to the door, and peered through the peephole. Kelly followed close behind her.

"Crap," Sophie muttered under her breath. She squared her shoulders and opened the door.

"Nick? I thought you were gone until tonight?" *Please don't let me have a giant neon sign on my forehead flashing "Jump my bones."*

Bailey barreled past her, leaping for her dad. If Bailey wanted something, apparently she had no problem going for it.

"Bailey, manners." The huge dog ignored him, her entire body wagging along with her tail.

"Wow, she definitely missed you." Sophie laughed, momentarily forgetting she'd nixed her questionable idea to have a fling with him.

Despite her kissing him the last time they were together. And dreaming about him. Because right now, he looked too tempting to resist. Oh, she was in trouble.

Nick brushed a kiss on her now heated cheek. "Hi, beautiful."

"Umm, Sophie?" Kelly waved a hand in Nick's direction.

She pasted on a smile. "Oh, sorry. Kelly, this is Nick Morgan, my landlord." She retreated a step and crossed her arms across her chest.

"Hi Kelly, that's me, the landlord." His lips twitched and he offered her one large tanned hand. "I take it you're up visiting from San Diego?"

"Yeah, I just arrived. Sophie didn't mention that you were so…um…young. I imagined some elderly caretaker." Kelly smirked.

"Elderly caretaker. Funny." He flashed his killer grin. "Sorry to interrupt. My meetings ended early in New York, so I caught an earlier flight."

Sophie leaned down to stroke Zack, who'd settled down next to her feet and attempted to ignore her best friend's probing gaze. Crap, no way would Kelly allow her to avoid all the questions once he left.

Kelly returned his smile. "Actually, Nick, you didn't interrupt. We were just catching up and figuring out our plans for the weekend. Any suggestions?"

"Oh, I can definitely show you a great time here." He flicked his gaze toward Sophie.

Sophie gritted her teeth. "No need. Alyssa already suggested a few spots—"

"Don't be silly," Kelly said. "Maybe Nick could be our tour guide and show us some must-see places? We'd like to check out a few art galleries, maybe have some sushi, visit a wine bar..."

Sophie's eyebrows almost flew off her forehead. What was her friend doing? Couldn't she see Sophie was attempting to distance herself from him? Time to stop this before it got any further.

She held up a hand. "That's okay. You must be tired from your trip, and I know you're busy. Maybe a few suggestions before you leave, though?"

*Subtle, girl, subtle.* Sophie didn't need a tour guide. She didn't need a man. She didn't need Nicholas Morgan. After their last two encounters ended in incredible kisses, she needed to get her hormones under control. If only her traitorous body would get on board with her resolve.

"I'd love to go. You know I wanted to see you again when I got back. I'll pick you up at seven, and we'll hit a great little wine bar and then the best sushi place in town." With a wink and another devastating grin, he backed out the door.

"Great. You're too kind. We'll see you then." Kelly waved goodbye before Sophie could protest.

The door shut with a decisive click, rendering his exit as dramatic as his entrance.

Sophie sailed past irritation into the world of aggravation. "What were you thinking? I don't want him to take us anywhere." Sophie crossed her arms across her chest and glowered at her friend.

Kelly's eyes widened. "Excuse me? I think you've been holding out on me here. The most gorgeous guy I've ever seen greets you with a kiss, and you fail to even mention his existence to me? Much less that the sparks flying off you two could ignite this whole cottage. Since when did you start keeping secrets? Spill it."

An expert in denial, Sophie could do a fine job of denying she had any interest whatsoever in Nick or his opinion on anything at all. Funny, she'd never held back anything from her best friend in the past.

She sighed. "I really didn't want to talk about it. You know, ostrich with the head in the sand and all that. It really is nothing. Classic scenario where the guy pursues the woman who isn't interested."

And she wasn't interested. Liar, liar.

Kelly barked out a laugh. "I know you, and you most definitely are attracted to him. You blushed like a virgin when he kissed you."

Sophie shrugged. Damn ivory complexion.

Kelly's expression sobered. "Why wouldn't you be interested? Because of Doug?"

Time to stop being such a child. Maybe she should stamp her foot while she was at it. "I can't deny I'm attracted to him. Who wouldn't be? We kissed…twice. My head almost exploded. The chemistry is like something out of some steamy romance novel."

Kelly crossed the room and enveloped her in a warm hug. She dropped her head on her friend's shoulder and squeezed her tight.

"I just want to heal and write my book. I don't need complications. He's a huge complication. I mean, the checkout girl at the grocery store told me he's known as the Player of Laguna, for god's sake."

Kelly stepped back and stared into her eyes. "Perfect. Maybe a fling is just what you need to move on. Nothing like some mind-blowing sex to erase memories of an ex. It might be a better idea than a year without men."

Her breath caught in her throat. "I just don't know if I'm ready or if I can handle him. He's just so…" Too good to be true.

Kelly rubbed her shoulder. "I'm sorry, I won't push it. If nothing else, he'll be a diversion tonight, right? Let's just enjoy our afternoon before we see him again."

SOPHIE CURSED at her closet again. Was it sheer vanity making her so particular about her outfit tonight?

Kelly laughed when she stepped into the bedroom. "Is that your whole wardrobe on the floor? Clothes crisis, I take it?"

"Yes, I'm pathetic. I need to look amazing, but I can't let him know I'm trying to look amazing. What should I wear?" Sophie tucked her hair behind her ear and grimaced at the mountain of clothes she'd tossed on the carpet.

Looking up, she did a double take. "You look incredible. Is that a new top? That shade of gold makes you look positively tawny. Meow."

Kelly grinned and waved a hand down the front of her body. "This old thing? Ha, yes, I got sucked into that new boutique at Del Mar Plaza last weekend. Isn't it great?"

Kelly pirouetted to the clothes pile and began pawing through, tossing items over her shoulder. She pounced on some black skinny jeans and an azure blue blouse with the tags still on it.

"Okay. Put this on." Kelly ripped off the tags and tossed her the shirt.

Her friend's bossiness always came in handy.

After she obeyed Kelly's order, Sophie smiled at her reflection. The top dipped slightly in front, hinting at cleavage while deepening and amplifying her blue eyes. Skinny jeans and towering stilettos provided a shot of confidence.

Kelly whistled. "You, my friend, are beautiful. The Player of Laguna won't know what hit him."

"I'm not trying to…" Sophie's protest sounded weak, even to her own ears.

Kelly held up a hand. "Please save it. I know you. Now you better make sure he doesn't come to your room and see this disaster."

"As if." Sophie huffed out a breath.

Of course, he wouldn't come anywhere near her bedroom.

Ever.

Maybe.

# CHAPTER 7

*W*hen the doorbell rang, Sophie yanked it open and promptly smacked into a brick wall.

"Ouch. Do you always stand so close to a door? You practically knocked the wind out of me." Her fingers grasped the brick wall's crisp button-down shirt and the heat from Nick's solid chest seared her fingers.

She retreated a step and clasped her hands behind her back, her heart hammering against her ribcage. *Must stop touching him.* What was it about this man that had her acting like a teenage girl at her first boy-band concert? She dug her fingernails into her palms.

His chiseled mouth quirked up on one side and he gestured to the porch. "I was just right here."

She glanced down and lo and behold––he did appear to be at a normal distance from the door. Drawing herself up to her full five feet six inches, she shrugged.

Kelly appeared beside her. "Okay, kids. Enough of this silliness. Nick, we're starving and ready to be wined and dined. Let's go."

"I'm parked right outside." Nick smiled.

They followed him to his sleek black sedan. "Let me open the door for you."

"Thank you, sir." Kelly hopped into the front seat of the car, leaving Sophie no choice but to sit in the back.

She settled into the comfortable backseat. She'd planned on avoiding him and here she was, spending another evening with him. And why was it annoying to be relegated to the backseat, like a kid? She stuck her tongue out at Mr. Persistent.

Nick's glance caught hers in the rearview mirror. Of course, he'd looked at the exact moment she'd given in to a childish impulse. His mouth quirked at the corners before he returned his focus to the road.

Not that she cared what he thought one way or the other. She was planning on being a single novelist for the foreseeable future.

Like Jane Austen.

Just like Jane Austen.

They arrived at Vines, a charming little wine bar. When the valet opened Sophie's door, she resolved to have a good time. After all, Kelly was here, and she'd be the perfect buffer.

Nick offered one arm to Kelly and his other arm to Sophie. Goosebumps erupted along her skin the moment her hand touched his hot sinewy forearm.

Music drifted through the open windows and humming conversation filled the intimate space. A high wood-beamed ceiling bestowed a feeling of warmth. The far wall was exposed brick with stenciled drawings depicting what appeared to be small Italian towns dotted across it.

"This is awesome," Kelly said. "Just our kind of place. Shall we grab a spot at the bar, or do you see an open table?"

An enormous polished mahogany bar occupied much of the room, and café tables were set amongst the wine racks. Clusters of young, attractive people chatted and sipped wine.

"Don't worry. I can get us a table." He raised his hand in the direction of the bar. A tall, handsome, dark-haired man waved him over. "I'll be right back."

Kelly gawked. "Wow, check out that bartender. Maybe I need to move up here to take advantage of all these beautiful men."

"What about Robert? Aren't you guys together?" Sophie frowned.

Kelly waved a hand and met Sophie's gaze. "Let me enjoy the scenery. Remember, I'm not discussing Robert on this visit. And Nick's on his way back over."

"Follow me." He led them to a table next to the garage-door-style windows that opened onto the street, bringing in the crisp evening air.

A lanky redhead approached, greeted Nick with a peck on the cheek, and left them menus. Settling into their chairs, they reviewed the extensive wine list, which featured both old and new-world vintages. Nick ordered a bottle of Chateauneuf-du-Pape for them along with a cheese-and-charcuterie board and some marcona almonds.

"Yum, all my favorite things." Kelly clapped her hands together. "So what's the hot bartender's story?"

Sophie's head snapped toward her friend. Before she could ask why she was scoping out the bar owner, Nick responded.

"Christian? He owns this place. He's an old friend, and he asked about you too." Nick smiled. "Do you want me to introduce you?"

"No, no, that's okay." Kelly shook her head.

The waitress returned and showed Nick the bottle. When she uncorked the wine, she poured for him first, but he deferred to Sophie. She swirled the wine to allow the aromas to release and approved of the moderate legs showing in the wineglass. Then, she inhaled the aroma and hmm'd at the notes of lavender and spice.

She held the first sip in her mouth, allowing the dense, bold flavors to explode on her tongue. When she looked at Nick, his eyes were narrow, and his jaw was tight. She loved wine and enjoyed the whole sensual process that comprised sampling. If he found that sexy, so be it. She nodded at the waitress, who filled their glasses and stepped away.

"You didn't tell me you were so into wine when we had dinner." Nick's intense stare pinned her to the spot.

Kelly sampled her wine. "Really? Sophie always picks the wine for us. She's got an amazing palate."

"Don't exaggerate." Heat flooded her cheeks. Between the constant blushing, fluttering, and shivering, maybe she did belong in a Jane Austen novel.

Nick shifted his attention to Kelly, and Sophie exhaled a steadying breath. "Tell me more about Sophie. She's full of surprises."

"Well, did you know that she loves romance novels? She's got a stack of those historical bodice rippers somewhere in your cottage. The old-school ones with Fabio on the cover…" Kelly fanned one hand in front of her face.

Sophie pointed at her BFF. Fabio wasn't on any of the covers, was he? "Stop, or I'm going to tell the hot bartender you want to take him home tonight."

"You wouldn't dare." Kelly's mouth snapped shut.

Nick leaned closer. "Really? Are you writing a romance novel?"

"Don't you worry about what I'm writing. Next subject, please."

Nick waggled his eyebrows. "Like pirates tossing wenches over their shoulders and—"

Sophie held up her hand, stemming a giggle. "No way. Discussion over."

"Fine, we'll leave the books alone for now. She also drives like a maniac. Did she tell you how she almost demolished one of your neighbor's hedges before she arrived?" Kelly snickered.

Kelly's new topic wasn't a big improvement. Usually, Sophie found her best friend hilarious. Not so much tonight.

"No, are you all right? Were you hurt?" Nick's tone sharpened and he grasped her hand.

A flicker of heat flashed up her arm. "Just my pride. Some truck came flying toward me, and the road is so narrow up there."

"You need to be careful—the road is treacherous." Concern filled his eyes, and his fingers tightened on hers.

"I'm fine. Nothing happened. Kelly drives like a grandma and thinks anyone who drives one mile over the speed limit is a drag racer. And can I have my hand back?" Sophie tugged at her hand, striving to keep the mood light. *What was up with his over-the-top reaction?*

Nick released her and sat back in his chair; his eyes chilled into chips of jade-green glass.

Just in time, the waitress returned with their appetizers. Kelly regaled them with entertaining stories about her law firm's stuffy coworkers. Sophie's shoulders softened as the earlier friction disappeared. She excused herself and headed to the ladies' room.

While in front of the mirror, Sophie reapplied nude-pink lip gloss and fluffed her hair. Her initial plan to remain single for a year suddenly seemed overly dramatic. Maybe getting under Nick would help her get over Doug once and for all.

Besides, she trusted Kelly's judgment completely and her friend liked him. Not all men were jerks like her ex–fiancé and her deadbeat dad. A rebound romance could help her find her confidence again––mind made up; she headed back to their table.

When Sophie wove through the crowd, she froze when she spotted a stunning brunette in her seat. Who the hell was she? The woman tossed her head and leaned against Nick, smashing her impressive cleavage into his side. Sophie's buoyant mood deflated, and jealousy licked at her belly.

Memories of Doug's infidelity slapped into her. She'd sworn never to be involved in a love triangle again. She'd overestimated her ability to handle a player. Celibacy was safer, after all. Donning her best poker face, she returned to the table.

"There she is." Kelly's smile was strained. "We were wondering when you'd get back. Are you almost ready to head out to sushi?"

"Whenever you are." Sophie wanted to bolt, but she wasn't about to reveal her cards.

A smiling Nick stood and gestured to the woman who remained in Sophie's chair. Didn't she see Sophie's wineglass?

"There you are. I want you to meet Heather, my right hand at work. Heather, meet my new tenant, Sophie."

Sophie sucked in a sharp inhale. *His tenant?* That's how Nick saw her? His rental income? A polite obligation?

Heather rose but made no move to vacate Sophie's spot. The woman's fake smile revealed blinding-white teeth––probably veneers––and didn't reach her glittering dark eyes. A flash of hostility flared before the woman could hide it. No way this woman was only his colleague.

Fine, she could have him. No more vacillation. Decision made.

The Player of Laguna was her landlord. Nothing more. Regardless of why he'd introduced her as his tenant, Sophie retreated to her original stance where Nick was concerned. Player. Definitely not her interim man.

Sophie reached for her wineglass and glanced around the

table. "Nice to meet you. Maybe you should stay and hang out, Nick. Kelly and I can head over to dinner if you'll just tell us where it is?"

A crease appeared between Nick's eyebrows. Clueless oblivious man.

"The reservations aren't for another half an hour," he shook his head. "Let's finish our wine first."

"Oh, please don't let me interrupt your evening. I was just headed back to my table." Heather wrapped scarlet-tipped talons around his forearm. "Lovely to meet you, girls. See you soon, Nick."

She strutted away from the table in her skin-tight leopard-print pencil skirt and fitted silk blouse, like a woman who was hyperaware of her beauty and who loved to flaunt it.

Kelly and Sophie exchanged glances, and as longtime best friends, no words were necessary. They'd both seen Heather's possessiveness and Nick's ease around the woman. If only she and Kelly could ditch him and go to dinner by themselves, but she refused to show she was affected. No way in hell would Nick discover she'd started to soften to the idea of jumping his bones.

For the remainder of the evening, she dug deep and continued to laugh and act lighthearted, despite the pit in her belly. At the sushi bar, she maneuvered so Kelly was sitting between her and Nick. It was easy to allow her outgoing friend to dominate the conversation and keep it casual.

Nick tried to catch her eye and draw her into the conversation. Not happening.

Mellow from the wine and Kelly's presence, Sophie maintained her nonchalant façade. Because Kelly rode in the front seat when he'd picked them up, it was simple to repeat the pattern. She managed to escape out of the car with a jaunty wave when Nick dropped them off at the house.

Now he had zero excuses to seek her out. She'd avoid him at all costs. The evening served as a reminder that she was here to create a new life as an independent woman and author. No more of this ridiculous flip-flopping over him.

No way Mr. Sex-on-a-Stick would distract her from her goals.

# CHAPTER 8

*N*ick had the attention span of a gnat this morning. Come to think of it, since Sophie moved into the cottage, he'd had the least productive few weeks he could recall. After the way she'd kissed him before he went to New York, he'd anticipated a very different reception. Hell, he'd hopped on an earlier flight to see her.

Then she'd frozen him out again at dinner. How could he keep up with Sophie's mercurial moods? He tossed his pencil down on his desk and stalked to the large picture window framing the incredible view of Laguna.

Screw the deadlines.

He texted his buddy Brandt, who was always ready to surf, any time of day. He grabbed his favorite surfboard from his quiver in the office closet and headed out the door. Until he cleared his mind, he wouldn't accomplish anything today.

Brandt texted that the waves were pumping at their favorite spot, Thalia Street, and to meet him there. When he arrived, the few parking spots on the ocean side were already full, indicating they weren't the only locals surfing instead of working. He parked across the street next to Brandt's Range

Rover and they changed into their wetsuits. They jogged across Pacific Coast Highway and descended the stairs onto the rocky beach.

"What's up?" Brandt asked as they strode into the pounding surf.

"Can't get any work done lately." Nick paddled out past the surf break. "Really need to soak my head."

He and Brandt rarely discussed their feelings. They'd been friends for years and shared similar views on dating and marriage. Dating was great. Marriage––not their gig.

But Sophie was different. Lately, everything reminded him of her. They bobbed in the surf, waiting for the next set of waves to roll in. Maybe Brandt would have some insight.

*Screw it.* "Well, actually there's this girl."

Brandt's head whipped toward him so fast he was surprised it didn't fly off. "What? You're asking me about a girl? Has hell frozen over? Nick Morgan lost his touch?"

"Shut up, man. This one's different. She's blowing hot and cold, and it's driving me crazy." What the hell was he saying? Brandt would never let him live it down.

Brandt chuckled. "Hot and cold, huh? Welcome to the real world."

"Oh right, like you'd know." His friend continued to hoot, and Nick willed a huge wave to come in and shut him up.

Shaking off the laughter, Brandt quirked a dark brow. "You are serious. Okay, well, maybe she just isn't into you. Can you introduce me?"

Nick paddled over toward Brandt, intending to knock him off his board, and simultaneously prayed for a shark to come snap up his friend. He settled for splashing him in the face, which silenced him for at least a moment as he shook the water out of his eyes.

"Forget it." He was losing his frickin' mind.

Brandt's eyes widened, and Nick turned his head toward

the open sea. A huge set approached, so he angled his board toward shore and paddled to catch a wave. He popped up and rode it in toward shore, reveling in the freedom.

They surfed for about an hour, and anytime Brandt opened his mouth, Nick cut him off by focusing on the waves. He was so not having this discussion. The healing salt air and sunshine warmed him, his muscles relaxed and his mind quieted.

Despite being out in the ocean, memories of the past unsettled him. After he and Alyssa had lost their when their parents had lost control of the car while on vacation in Ireland, they'd become incredibly close. Because both of their parents had no siblings, Nick had stepped into the dual role of brother and father.

He sheltered his little sister--his only family. The only woman who held a piece of his heart. She complained that his protectiveness created a tough barrier to her potential relationships.

And yeah, it wasn't like he'd formed any serious long-term relationships. It was simpler that way. For some reason, his attraction to Sophie was triggering unwelcome insights. She piqued his curiosity despite himself.

If another woman had played the fire and ice routine, he would've hightailed it the other way. But something about her made him want to delve beneath the surface. Damn it, once he wanted something, he never stopped until he got it.

And he wanted Sophie Barnes.

When they headed in, Brandt said, "Seriously bro, you seem bummed. Let's grab a beer tonight."

"Thanks, I'll let you know." He waved a hand and changed back into his work clothes. He wasn't going to give up on Sophie.

When Nick entered his office, Heather was behind his desk, rifling through some papers.

"Hi, boss. Were you out at an important board meeting?" She smiled at the inside term surfers used for a midday surf break. "I've got some correspondence to review with you before our hospital board meeting. I made reservations at Splashes for lunch so we can kill two birds with one stone."

Lunch with Heather at the world-renowned Surf and Sand Hotel restaurant didn't appeal, but they did have to review the plans and cement the strategy for the upcoming meeting. And at least it would distract him from obsessing over Sophie.

He shrugged. "Sure, let's walk over."

SOPHIE AND KELLY strolled down the Pacific Coast Highway or "PCH" as the locals called the picturesque coastal road. Sophie savored the last drop of salted caramel gelato from her spoon and dropped it back into the paper cup.

She licked her lips. "That was the most delicious gelato ever, even for breakfast. Okay, back to the other night, now tell me, what's the deal with ogling the hot bar owner? Did you break up with Robert?"

Kelly wrinkled her nose. "I wouldn't say we broke up... He's just been acting weird lately, and I'm sick of it. Coming to see you and having some separation will hopefully give me some perspective. When I'm ready to talk about it, I will. And that guy was gorgeous."

"Yes, he was. But could you ever leave the firm? Move up here?" Wouldn't that be a dream come true?

Kelly waved a hand. "You never know. The family firm's tough to escape. Anyway, what happened Friday night? Because even when you froze Nick out, he couldn't take his eyes off you. I don't get the problem with going for it."

Sophie blew out a breath. "I can talk a big game about

jumping his bones but seeing that woman wrapped around him triggered me. I can't risk getting involved with another player."

Kelly gave her a one-arm hug. "He's not Doug, and he's not your dad. Take your time, but don't let the past control your future. I think getting your mojo back is important. Just lay out the ground rules and have a fling."

"We'll see. Now help me buy something cute before you head home." Maybe her best friend was right.

They spent the morning window-shopping in the plethora of charming boutiques. Kelly was hip and stylish and although Sophie tended to live in her yoga capris these days, it couldn't hurt to look, right?

When they exited one store with prices only royalty could afford, Sophie caught sight of a tall guy with slicked-back damp hair and a perfect ass. Her breath caught in her throat––Nick was across the street.

Seriously? Maybe this town was too small. Then she noticed the brunette with him. Heather. No way did she want another encounter with them.

"Hey Kel, I think I need to get to work. I shouldn't spend money on clothes anyway. And you need to head back soon too, right?" Sophie grabbed her friend's arm and took off at a fast trot toward the car.

Kelly gave her the side-eye. "Okay, okay, no need to run."

They reached Kelly's car and Sophie sighed once Kelly eased out into traffic. Confrontation dodged. Time to bury herself in creating a fictional world where she controlled external events.

Brakes screeched, metal crunched, glass shattered, and her head whacked into the headrest. What the hell? Sophie jerked her head up just in time to see them slam into the back of a truck's bumper. The impact knocked her toward the dashboard.

Everything went still. An eerie silence filled the air. Sophie reached up with a trembling hand and touched her head. Yes, it was still attached to her body. She turned to see her friend immobile, staring into space.

"Are you okay? Kelly, answer me." She reached for Kelly's hand.

Kelly turned, her eyes glazed, her face a sickly green, glistening with sweat. "What happened? I just pulled out and I don't know what happened…"

Oh no, her friend looked ready to puke. Time to exit the car. Fast.

Sophie unbuckled her seatbelt—thank god for the seatbelt—and opened the door. "We're okay, we're okay, come on, let's get out of the car and see the damage."

Her legs wobbled like a newborn colt's. The crinkled hood of the compact car spewed smoke, crushed into the bumper of the black truck in front. A big green sedan's bumper was practically hooked on the car's flattened rear. Tiptoeing over shattered glass, Sophie picked her away toward the driver's side door.

Sophie yanked open the door, where Kelly sat frozen and eased her out of her seat. "Come on, let's get out. You're going to be fine."

Kelly looked far from fine.

Horns honked from the traffic stuck behind the pileup and angry drivers shouted, drowning out her friend's feeble reply.

"Sophie," a deep voice shouted.

She glanced up and Nick sprinted toward them from across the street, his brow furrowed.

"Oh my god, are you okay?" He reached for her. "Someone call 911," he directed the small group of gawking bystanders.

"We don't need an ambulance. We just need to get out of

the road." Sophie ignored his hand and guided Kelly to an empty bench on the far end of the sidewalk. Kelly sank onto the bench and dropped her head between her legs.

She rubbed circles on Kelly's back. "Just breathe, we're fine. Everything is fine. It was just a fender bender."

Nick stood in front of them, his tanned face pale, moisture beaded on his forehead. "Please tell me you're okay. Please let me help."

"I think we're fine. Maybe you could get our purses out of the car and call the police?"

"Of course, of course, I'll take care of it. Just stay where you are." Nick charged back toward the accident site.

An hour later they'd given a police report, watched the accordion-like remnants of Kelly's car towed away, and checked each other for signs of serious wounds. Once Nick was satisfied neither of their injuries necessitated a visit to the hospital, he bundled them into his car and drove them home.

Back at the cottage, Sophie set Kelly up in her bed, plumped the pillows, and tucked in the lace coverlet. "Just rest for a few hours. I'll check on you."

When Sophie returned to the living room, Nick sat on the couch, his elbows on his knees, his head in his hands.

"Nick?" She'd figured he'd have headed back to work after bringing them home.

He patted the couch next to him. Not knowing what else to do, she sat.

Nick clasped her hands and gazed into her eyes. "You scared me. The crash sounded like a bomb exploded. I thought I'd lost you."

*Lost her*? What?

Heat curled down her spine from his intense gaze. Time to defuse his attention. "I'm fine, just shaken up and a couple bruises—not a big deal. I'm more worried about Kelly. Her car's totaled, and she's already a nervous driver."

He pulled her into a hug and stroked his strong hands down her back. An involuntary shiver racked her body. Where was this affection coming from?

He shifted back. "Well, let me know what I can do to help."

"That's sweet of you but I think we're good. So…" Yeah, between the warmth from his skin, his clean masculine scent, and the concern on his gorgeous face, she was burning up.

Nick raked one hand through his thick tawny hair. "Look, I'll just put it out there. I can't stop thinking about you and I really want to get to know you better. Will you let me take you out again and we can see if the third time's the charm?"

Her heart started galloping in her chest. Hadn't she decided to take the safe road? No rebound? This caring, sweet side of him could drop her from simple lust to full-blown infatuation. Fast.

Right now, Nick signaled danger: Too kind. Too handsome. Too everything.

"I've wanted to see that new Quentin Tarantino movie. Wanna go tomorrow night?" Nick smiled.

A movie. A date. A safe date. An opportunity to hang out, without the distraction of their over-the-top chemistry. Could she handle it?

"I'm putting Kelly on the train tomorrow morning, so, sure, as long as we can get a giant bucket of popcorn and some peanut M&Ms." Her favorite snack.

His lips twitched. "That's pretty specific. You want both?"

"Well, I've created the perfect combination. You put the peanut M&Ms into the popcorn. It's the perfect blend of salty and sweet. You'll love it." *Keep the conversation light-hearted.*

"Whatever you want. I'll pick you up at six thirty. And if

that isn't enough dinner, we can always grab a bite afterward." Nick laughed.

She returned his grin. "Perfect."

He clasped her chin and brushed a feather-light kiss against her lips. "See you tomorrow, beautiful."

And, yes, her heart skipped a beat.

# CHAPTER 9

*S*ophie checked on Kelly, who was sleeping with Zack curled up at her side. Satisfied her BFF was resting comfortably, she quietly pulled the bedroom door shut.

Stretching her arms overhead, she grimaced at the stiffness setting in from the accident. Time to take advantage of the quiet and percolate on the situation with Mr. Nicholas Morgan. And what better place to do it than in a long hot bath?

Once she'd settled into the tub, complete with fragrant bubbles and a yogurt face mask, she closed her eyes and dropped her head back onto the bath pillow. The silky water caressed her skin, and the warmth soothed her muscles. Heaven.

A moment later, her phone rang. When she glanced at the display, Nick's number popped up. Already?

"Hi beautiful, what are you up to?" His voice was husky.

Her breath hitched. "I'm up to my collarbone in bubbles. You?"

He exhaled a deep breath. "Seriously? You're killing me, Sophie. I can be there in five minutes?"

"What happened to getting to know each other? Taking it slow?" The heat in the bathtub ratcheted up about fifty degrees--she fanned her face with one hand.

Nick chuckled. "I'm only teasing, I wanted to check in on you and Kelly. Are you sure you're still okay?"

Sophie's chest tightened. "I'm okay. She's sleeping and will be fine. Thanks again for all your help—you've been amazing."

"You're sure there's nothing you need?"

Besides you here to wash my back? "Yes, I'm sure."

"Now tell me if those bubbles have started to melt?" he whispered.

"We are so not discussing my bubble bath. I'll see you tomorrow." Warmth pooled low in her belly.

"Good night, beautiful."

She hung up, her eyelids fluttered shut, and she settled back into the steamy water. Okay, no question their chemistry was scorching and no question now that she would succumb to temptation. A fling with Nick was just what she needed.

A few moments later, the phone rang again. The man was nothing if not persistent. Without opening her eyes, Sophie reached for her phone. "No, you are not joining me in the bubble bath."

"Sophie."

She jolted upright, and water splashed over the tub's edge. Unable to suppress the bile rising in her throat, her fingers curled around the phone. Only one man had that smug, superior tone.

"Doug, what do you want?" she said, her voice flat.

"Sophie, I've missed you so much. How are you, baby?" Her ex-fiancé crooned.

Her fingers trembled, and a chill flashed down her spine, despite the hot bath water. "Baby? Are you kidding me right now? How dare you call me? What part of you stood me up at the altar gives you the nerve to contact me?"

"Wait, please let me have a chance to explain everything. I screwed up. I got scared. I've had time to figure it all out and must see you--"

Her stomach heaved. "No, there's nothing you can say to change how you betrayed me."

"I messed up. But I love you so much, and I've figured it all out now. I've been going to therapy. I know I'd never cheat again. Please give me another chance. It can be like it was those first three years—incredible. You're the only one for me."

Tears streamed down her cheeks. Doug had gone to therapy? He sounded so sincere--like the man she'd fallen in love with years ago. She'd loved him with all her heart.

"Are you still there? Please tell me where you are so I can come talk to you in person. Please believe me that I love you so much and I'll never hurt you again."

Sophie's nostrils flared. *Bullshit.* He was full of it. She'd heard his excuses before. Never again. One and done.

"It's too late. I don't love you anymore. Lose the number, and while you're at it, stop harassing people to find out where I am. I am no longer any of your concern."

She hurled the phone across the bathroom, where it smashed against the wall with a satisfying crack. Too bad it wasn't that asshole's head.

Scalding tears of pain and rage poured down her cheeks as the past flooded back. The water chilled, and she dragged herself out of the tub, managing to wrap herself in a fluffy towel. Unsteady and queasy, she sank onto the thick bathroom rug, curling into a tight ball, and flashed back.

The first few years together everything seemed perfect.

They were blissful, always laughing, having fun, traveling, enjoying each other's company. Sophie had believed she was with her soul mate, her ride-or-die.

After the engagement, things shifted gradually. Doug's excuses of having to work late, his growing travel schedule, his increased aloofness, and their correspondingly decreased sex life. He'd blamed it all on work. She'd trusted him—eager to believe that once they were married, they'd rekindle the romance.

Yeah, she'd been naïve and blind. It wasn't Doug's career. Nope, he'd been leading a double life––sleeping with another woman the entire time they'd been engaged. For months he'd lied to her and continued to move forward with wedding plans.

Who does that?

Why did he even bother to propose?

Sadness, despair, and the overwhelming feeling she'd never be enough consumed her. His betrayal shot her back to when she was five years old, when her father had strolled out the door without a backward glance.

Sophie wrapped her arms around her waist and rocked herself until her breathing slowed. She'd go sleep on the couch. In a minute.

"Sophie?"

She cracked open an eye. Kelly peered down at her from the bathroom doorway. What the…

Lifting a hand to her pounding head, she groaned. It felt like she'd spent the evening at a wild bachelorette party in Las Vegas, without the dancing, drinking, and fun. She must've passed out on the floor.

"Sophie," Kelly repeated. "Are you okay? Why'd you sleep in the bathroom? Do you have a concussion?"

Sophie turned her head from side to side, just in case. "It certainly feels like my brain imploded, but no, no concussion."

She spotted her phone, praying it hadn't shattered when she'd hurled it across the room. Rising to her feet, she picked it up, with a blessing for the pint-sized computer nerd at the cell phone store who'd insisted she buy a hardcover case. She'd cracked the front of the phone, but the familiar symbol appeared when powered it on.

Kelly scrubbed her hands across her face. "Okay, you need to catch me up. What happened to your phone?"

"Coffee first." Desperate for caffeine, she started toward the kitchen with Kelly on her heels.

Kelly sank onto a kitchen stool while Sophie brewed coffee. "Did yesterday really happen?"

"Yeah, your car is totaled. Are you feeling better today?" Hopefully, Kelly felt better than she did right now.

Kelly's brows drew together. "I'm fine. The accident freaked me out, but physically I'm okay. Are you sure you are?"

"I will be. Doug called me last night."

Kelly slammed her hands down on the kitchen counter. "What? Are you kidding me right now? Why won't he leave you alone?"

Sophie outlined the short call, punctuated with hisses and disbelieving snorts from her best friend. Her shoulders softened as Kelly mirrored her outrage and commiserated with her. In the harsh morning light, Doug's call voice didn't seem as harrowing as it had in the dark.

But no way was she healthy enough to start a new relationship––not even a landlord with benefits. Not even close. Talk about a wake-up call.

She handed Kelly a mug and inhaled the first healing sip of her own. "Well, there's one more thing I need to share."

Kelly gestured with her coffee for her to continue.

"Nick checked in again yesterday. He asked if we could start over, go to the movies…"

"Go. Absolutely go. It's perfect timing."

"I don't know. I'm afraid I'm too much of a mess, and he is intense. It isn't fair to either of us for me to get involved with him." She sighed and pushed her hair out of her face.

Kelly shook her head. "He's a great guy—he was wonderful yesterday after the accident. He's also a big boy. He pursued you. And you said he's known as Player of Laguna so it's not like he's looking for something serious either. Just be honest that you need to go slow. You told him about Doug, right?"

Sophie sipped her coffee, keeping her gaze averted.

"Right? Sophie, you haven't told him about the wedding?"

Sophie ran her tongue around her teeth. "Well, when the heck was I going to tell him? He just takes…I don't know, he just takes charge, and I didn't manage to bring it up."

"You need to tell him. You said you're going to the movies tonight? Tell him before you go. Or heck, afterward. Just tell him tonight. If you're going to date him, even casually, he deserves to know you've recently gone through a breakup and aren't here just because of the book."

"Okay, okay…enough about that." She'd avoided his questions about her reasons for moving before because she wasn't ready to open that can of worms. "Are you sure you don't want me to drive you back? The train's okay?"

"Okay, I'll drop it for now. But I really do want to get a restraining order against Doug. I don't trust him." A crease appeared between Kelly's brows. "And I'll take the train. I don't want to be in a car for a bit. Thanks, though."

AFTER DROPPING Kelly off at the train station, Sophie headed to the yoga studio in an attempt to quiet her racing thoughts with some sweaty yoga.

She managed to slide in the door before it closed. Alyssa waved from across the room. Oh crap. Alyssa.

She was contemplating hooking up with Alyssa's brother. Talk about awkward.

Would it impact their budding friendship? How the heck had everything gotten so complicated when she'd moved up to Laguna to simplify her life?

Fortunately, the teacher invited them to close their eyes and focus on their breath. Time to push aside her obsessive thoughts and focus on creating some calm inside. At least for an hour.

After class, Alyssa approached her. "Hey, how are you? Nick told me about the accident. Do you have time to grab a juice or even a bite at the bistro?"

"Hi, I'm fine, just a few bruises. I've got some catching up to do on my writing schedule. I don't have time for breakfast, but I can grab a juice at the juice bar." Maybe the antioxidants would repair the brain cells she seemed to have lost.

Alyssa entertained her with some funny snippets about last night's terrible date. Apparently, the guy showed up in skin-tight acid-washed jeans à la Bon Jovi circa 1985, complete with a ripped tank top and black eyeliner. He'd evidently used a photo from twenty years prior on his online dating profile. Nice.

After sharing stories about their favorite nostalgic hair-band concerts—when Alyssa had been in elementary school, mind you--Alyssa had escaped under the pretext of an early work appointment.

How could someone as gorgeous and clever as Alyssa

have a challenging time finding a partner? Were there any good guys out there?

Was Nick one of the good guys?

Would she be better off as the crazy old cat lady living with twenty cats and piles of books? Because right now she was careening down the fast track...

# CHAPTER 10

*N*ick arrived right on time, looking gorgeous in faded jeans and a white T-shirt. How did he always manage to kickstart butterflies in her stomach? Just by standing there with the setting sun framing him? She was in trouble.

He clasped her face in his hands and planted a soft kiss on her lips. "Hi beautiful, ready to go?"

Unable to resist, Sophie wound her arms around his neck and deepened the kiss. His strong arms banded around her waist, pressing her against his broad chest.

"Mmm, feel free to greet me like that every time I come over." He lifted his head, his eyes hooded.

Heat flooded her cheeks, and she retreated a step. "Let's go. Prepare to be blown away by the movie snack of the century."

Determined to keep things light before "the talk," Sophie swallowed the lick of panic bubbling in her gut. She'd accomplished next to nothing all afternoon, instead wrestling with how much to share about Doug.

The angel on her shoulder whispered "tell him everything" because if they were going to have any kind of relationship, even friends-with-benefits, honesty and trust were essential.

The devil urged her to zip it. What if he lived up to his Player of Laguna reputation and simply wanted a fling? They'd only known each other a few weeks. What if she scared him off with a premature talk?

"Is that a blush? Popcorn à la Sophie is that decadent?" His lips twitched.

"Just a little warm, that's all. And yes, it's decadent." Damn fair skin betrayed her every time.

After they arrived at the luxury theater, they settled into their reclining seats, and Sophie poured peanut M&Ms into a tub of popcorn large enough to feed a family of four. When Nick sampled her concoction, his eyes closed in pleasure, and they dug in. He kept her hand clasped in his, and she lost herself in the dark humor of the film. The evening seemed normal. Simply a happy couple at the movies.

When they returned to her cottage, Nick walked her to the door and paused. Waiting on a signal from her.

"Come in, there's something I need to talk about with you." Her stomach roiled, all the candy and popcorn mixing with her jangled nerves.

He followed her inside and Zack offered his moral support––rubbing against her and purring like a motorboat.

Nick caught one hand, tugged her close, and brushed his lips against hers. "That sounds serious. Everything okay?"

She ducked out of his arms and headed to the couch. His touch scrambled her brain and stymied her best intentions. Perching on the sofa's edge, she motioned for him to sit on the far end. Sweat prickled on the back of her neck.

"I don't know how to even bring this up or if I even should bring it up at all. But I need to be honest with you about my past…" She sucked in an enormous breath and slowly released it.

His brows drew together. "Your past?"

Her heart hammered like she'd hiked Mt. Everest without a training plan. "First, I want to reiterate that I'm not trying to lead you on. I'm not playing games."

"Okay…" Nick's expression was unreadable.

"So you asked me before why I left San Diego and holed up in the cottage. There was more to it than just being ready to write my book." She paused and cleared her now-parched throat. "Actually, things were pretty traumatic and I kind of ran away."

He gestured with one hand for her to continue.

"I was engaged, and my fiancé jilted me at the altar. I left because I didn't want to face anyone, especially my ex. He's a total ass."

His bottle-green eyes narrowed. "Did he hurt you?"

She shook her head. "No, no, not how you think. He wasn't physically abusive. But he was a pathological liar. After he failed to show up for the wedding, I learned he'd been having an affair for almost a year."

"Sophie, I—"

She held up a hand. "Let me finish. Please. So I quit my job, dug into my savings, and decided I wouldn't date for a year and concentrate solely on writing my book. You'd be better off not getting involved with me."

Nick leaned forward. "We're already involved. That asshole sounds like he did a number on you. You're the most amazing woman I've ever met."

"Yeah, that's what he used to say too. But obviously something was wrong, or he wouldn't have cheated." A wave of sadness filled her. "I'd understand if you bailed. I'm just not sure if the timing is right."

"Sophie." He shifted across the couch, pulled her onto his lap, and snuggled her into the circle of his powerful arms.

She buried her face into the warm skin on the hollow of his throat. His clean masculine scent was incredible, and his hot hard body burned into her.

"Your ex is a prick. It's him, not you," he murmured against her hair. "I think you're incredible, and I'd like to keep seeing you."

Sophie nestled in closer, pressing her face into his neck as she nodded. "Yes."

He shifted back and gazed into her eyes. "If we're together, we aren't with anyone else."

Hope fluttered inside her. "Of course not."

Nick wrapped one hand into her hair and slanted his mouth across hers. His tongue stroked against hers, their breath mingling. With a moan, she wrapped her arms around his neck. His rigid length dug into her bottom, and his grip tightened in her hair. Heat curled down her spine, and her mind simply shut down.

She caressed the hot skin on the back of his neck which echoed the answering fire burning inside her. She scraped her nails down to his shoulders.

He growled low in his throat, pulled her up from the couch, and swept her into his arms. He gazed down at her, his eyes hooded. "I want you. Please, can I have you?"

*Holy crap.* Nobody had ever picked her up as if she were light as a feather. His powerful arms cradled her as if he would never let go. "Nick...I don't..."

"Don't think. Just feel. Let me make love with you." He lowered his head and grazed the sensitive spot on the side of her neck.

Goosebumps erupted on her skin and shivers shot down her spine.

All she wanted was more.

More Nick.

He shifted his mouth back to hers, capturing her lips in a passionate kiss. Her goosebumps settled into a tingling that traveled down to her toes.

"Nick—" Sophie murmured against his mouth, "I don't just sleep with guys I barely know…"

"I know that. You know what we have is different. Do you want me tonight?" He nibbled along her jaw.

"Yes, I want you tonight." More than she'd wanted anything or anyone before.

Triumph flared in his eyes, and he carried her to her bedroom. He placed her on the bed and settled on top of her, his weight supported on his forearms. His hands cradled either side of her face and he deepened the kiss.

She couldn't breathe. Not because of his weight on top of her, which felt incredible. She simply couldn't suck in enough oxygen because all she wanted to do was inhale him. To throw caution to the wind and forget responsibility.

The crisp evening breeze glided through the bedroom window, bathing them in coolness. But nothing, not even the ocean air, could diffuse the flame burning between them.

Nick lifted his head, and even in the dim light, the intensity of his gaze scorched her. His strong fingers shifted the straps off her shoulders and down around her arms–– holding her immobile. She shivered.

"I have to taste you, Sophie." He planted a light kiss on her collarbone, then traveled south leaving a trail of fire along her skin.

He tugged down the top of her lacy pink bra and blew softly on her nipple. He gazed up at her through the tuft of hair falling over his forehead.

She held her breath when he lowered his head and kissed her nipple. Hard. Then he used his teeth. Her hips bucked and slammed into his. With her hands pinned to her sides, she couldn't move, and sensation flooded through her. Nick lifted his head again and flashed a wicked grin.

"Like that?" Without waiting for a response, he repeated the favor on her other breast. Her last sliver of control evaporated. She moaned his name.

He unhooked her bra and set her arms free. With one hand, he grabbed her wrists and held them over her head as he lowered his mouth to her breasts once more. Her nipples ached, shooting sensation to her core. Nick's talented mouth was driving her to the brink of coming apart.

Freeing her hands, his hot mouth traveled lower, taking his sweet time.

When he pulled down her matching lace thong, her fingers dug into the sheets, and she managed to suppress a scream. He nuzzled her, then licked her like an ice cream cone. Nudging her legs farther apart with his shoulders, he kissed and teased and drove her beyond reason. Her head dropped back onto the pillows, and she abandoned herself to the heat consuming her.

"I'm going to make you come right now." He thrust one thick finger inside her, then two. His skillful tongue never stopped, and waves of sensation poured through her. She dug her fingers into his thick, silky hair and rocked against him. Lights sparked behind her eyes, her back bowed, and she exploded with the biggest orgasm she'd ever experienced.

Floating, she was floating.

He rose above her, and her lips curved, bursting with pleasure. Yet, she wanted more. Needed more. She wanted all of him. She reached up and brushed her fingertips down his washboard abs. Cupped his impressive erection through his pants.

Nick was fully dressed, and she was totally naked. Not fair. She unbuckled his belt.

His breath caught and he rolled off the bed in one smooth

motion. He whipped off his belt, stepped out of his jeans, revealing male physical perfection. The statue of David had nothing on him––sweat gleamed on his tanned skin, emphasizing his sinewy muscles.

She licked her lips, eager for more. He pulled a foil packet out of his back pocket and tugged it open with his teeth.

He rejoined her and captured her mouth. Limbs heavy, she ran her hands down his back, raked his smooth skin with her nails, and savored his sharp intake of breath.

She'd die if he stopped kissing her.

Tongues tangled. Limbs intertwined. Passion ignited even hotter.

"I can't wait any longer, Sophie. I have to have you now." He nudged her knees apart and knelt between her legs. Together, they rolled on the condom, and he plunged into her in one powerful stroke.

Her breath caught in her throat as she worked to accommodate his thickness. "Give me a minute. Oh god, you are huge."

"Sophie." Nick held himself taut. His forehead pressed into hers as they adjusted to being connected. Exhaling in an enormous sigh, she smiled at the sensation of fullness.

He began to move, and she instinctually matched his rhythm. As they rocked together, she wrapped her legs around him, digging her heels into his back. Their breath came in harsh pants, their skin slick and hot. Everything fell away except for sheer pleasure and connection.

Nick clasped her face in his large hands, his eyes hooded. "Come for me again, Sophie. Now."

His demand shot straight to her center and with his name on her lips, she came apart. Again.

Nick followed her over with a groan.

After a few moments, she wasn't sure if she could feel her legs—or anything below her neck, for that matter. Not that she wanted to move, even if she could. Not after the most incredible sex she'd ever experienced. Nick hadn't moved and his weight on top of her was delicious. Solid.

A sharp pain shot up her calf muscle, bursting her bubble. She wiggled underneath him, but he remained immobile.

"Nick." Sophie caressed his back. When he didn't respond, she smacked his perfect ass.

"You're crushing me. Can you scoot off please?"

With a groan, he rolled off and sauntered to the bathroom to take care of the condom. When he returned, he pulled her back against his front and wrapped his strong arms around her. He sighed and pressed a kiss into her hair.

She melted.

Nicholas Morgan was a cuddler.

What a lovely surprise. His passion and stamina weren't unexpected, but his tenderness, his intense attention to her pleasure, and his sensitivity were.

Doug and her prior boyfriends hadn't been spooners. Not necessarily wham bam thank you ma'am, but not this possessive, wonderful warmth against her back.

Despite savoring the feel of him, a sliver of unease slid down her spine——what had happened to her one-year dating moratorium? What would the morning bring?

# CHAPTER 11

$\mathcal{N}$ick woke early to head to a work meeting. Sophie looked beautiful as she slept, the anxiety he'd seen on her face last night erased. He brushed a strand of silky dark hair away from her face and kissed her good-bye. With an unintelligible murmur, she rolled over and burrowed deeper into her pillow.

When he ran home to shower and change for a meeting with the hospital board, he couldn't dispel the uneasy sensation in his gut. It troubled him how negative she'd sounded, how doubtful about her own worth and beauty. The guy had obviously played a number on her. How could she take any blame for her ex-fiancé being such a two-timing piece of shit?

There was a guy code, at least a guy code for his friends. None of them would ever have carried on two relationships while planning to marry one of the women. If you were serious enough to propose to someone, to have a wedding planned, you followed through with your word. Hell, even in his nonexclusive relationships he'd only dated one woman at a time but had never considered anything long-term. Until Sophie.

Before Sophie, he'd stayed true to the vow he made to himself when his parents died. No way would he be vulnerable enough to have his heart ripped out again.

Before Sophie, he'd never felt a deep connection with a woman besides his sister.

But from the moment he'd witnessed the raw anguish on Sophie's face the day he'd come up to the cottage, it had triggered his own deeply buried heartache. Tugged at him.

In the past, if a woman had shared the fresh emotional trauma she'd suffered, he'd have done one of two things: turned tail and run or kept things straight sex.

Impossible with Sophie.

His chest tightened. No way could he stop seeing her now. Nor could he detach his emotions and keep their relationship physical.

Not that he was a guy who spent a lot of time analyzing his feelings. But he'd found himself daydreaming about her. Visions of the future included her, the unfamiliar urge to protect her, and the need to see her all the time. When she'd told him about her ex, he'd fantasized about hunting the guy down and making him pay for the way he'd treated her.

But what if she still hung up on her ex? Was he the rebound guy? Everyone knew how that usually turned out. Damn it, Sophie was different. Wasn't she?

He worked to ignore the niggling in the back of his brain.

Therein lay the problem––she'd just arrived in Laguna. Yet, their connection started the first day he saw her muttering to herself in front of the cottage. When he'd helped her up, the heat between them had shocked him.

Something tightened in his chest––he was falling in love with her. It was fast. It made no sense, but no woman had ever engaged him body, mind, and soul like this. Like his parents had been together. They had been madly in love, even after twenty-five years of marriage. Always a touch of the hand or a caress, always laughing and smiling with each other, always supportive in challenging or difficult times.

Dying together in the fiery car crash was probably no coincidence. Nick doubted one could have survived without the other. Was that what was happening with him and Sophie?

Just his luck to meet a woman who had him considering a real relationship and she was on the rebound. The timing sucked. Time—time was the answer. Friendship.

The day-to-day. Romance. He didn't want to scare her away, so he'd go slow. Where to begin?

Flowers, of course. Flowers. He'd send her a huge bouquet—women loved flowers. He'd romance her and hold back on the physical side—even if it killed him—and show her he was one of the good guys, a worthy partner. He'd demonstrate he truly loved her.

*Shit.* He loved her. His chest tightened as the epiphany hit him. He wanted to marry Sophie. He wanted her to be his forever.

"Marriage." Even saying the word out loud didn't cause him to break into a cold sweat. Terror didn't overwhelm him. Instead, energy surged through him, a desire to show her they belonged together.

Starting right now.

He picked up the phone and dialed the florist down the street.

# CHAPTER 12

When Sophie woke she reached out and the sheets next to her were cool. Nick was gone. A vague memory of him kissing her at some ungodly hour this morning flashed through her. She stretched her arms overhead, enjoying the lingering soreness in her muscles.

None of her steamy romance novels prepared her for the real deal. He was the most amazing lover she'd ever had. No pirate fantasy needed.

But she wished he'd stayed for coffee so she could see how her revelations had affected him. Affected them. The conversation had been tough. Being vulnerable wasn't her forte, but she'd delved into her inner strength. Honesty and trust were vital. No space existed for secrets between them.

Her cheeks flamed recalling how after he'd asked to keep seeing her and to be exclusive, he'd swept her off her feet. And taken her to bed. So at least for last night, they'd been okay.

It was a new day. Time to get down to business and start putting pencil to paper. Or more accurately fingers to keyboard. Although that didn't have the same ring to it.

When she was pouring her first cup of coffee, her phone rang. When she checked the screen, she grimaced. Crap, her mother. Could she handle a dose of Martine Monceau this morning? She took a fortifying breath and answered.

"Sophie, I'm so glad I caught you. I'll be there in a few hours, and I've made lunch reservations at Splashes."

She rolled her eyes. "Did you consider I might be busy for lunch?" Just like her mother to make plans without consulting her first.

"Busy? You quit your job, ran away to play at being a writer, you have no man—what could you possibly be doing? I'm heading to L.A., and I want to see my only daughter." Her mother managed to inject a note of hurt into her accented voice.

Sophie counted to three. "I'm not playing at anything, Mom. You know writing is my new career…"

"Non, non. Let's not argue. Please be realistic, and you've got to be practical. We'll discuss your return to San Diego and a new job opportunity I've found for you. Meet me at eleven thirty."

"I'm not going back to San Diego… Mom?" Her mother had hung up. Without listening to a word she said—nothing new.

Sophie sighed and headed to take a shower. At least she had a few hours to build her defenses before the onslaught. Because it was easier to polish up for her Mom than listen to criticisms about her appearance, she took extra care with her makeup.

While she perused her closet, the doorbell rang. Crap, didn't her mom say to meet at the restaurant?

Her formerly languorous muscles tightened. What if Doug ignored her and showed up? Holding her breath, she peered through the peephole.

Sophie's shoulders softened. A young boy sporting a

backward baseball cap, slouchy jeans, and an enormous bouquet of flowers stood on her doorstep.

Had Doug somehow found her and was now sending flowers, his usual MO when he'd messed up? Well, except for the ultimate mess-up at the end—no flowers had accompanied the abandonment at the altar. But this colorful bouquet wasn't her ex's customary two-dozen pink roses, so who knew.

Bemused, she accepted the flowers from the gangly teenage boy and carried the bouquet into the kitchen. A vibrant mix of sunflowers, bird-of-paradise, and violet-colored accents, it was like a burst of tropical sunlight. She sniffed the fragrant blooms and happiness sparkled inside her.

She ripped the envelope open. *"Thanks for being such a bright ray of sunshine. Nick."*

She hugged the card to her chest and two-stepped around the kitchen. Cracking open one eye, Zack watched her joyous dance. Wow. Flowers just because. Not for an apology, not for a birthday, not for an anniversary. Just because he was thinking of her.

Without hesitation, she dialed his cell to thank him.

"Hello, Nick's phone," a woman's voice purred.

Sophie's glanced at the screen to make sure she hadn't called his office number. Nope, it was his cell. "Umm, can I please speak to Nick?"

"Can I tell him who's calling? He's in a meeting right now." Was this Heather answering his cell phone? It was one thing for her to be answering the office phone, but his personal cell?

"Of course, it's Sophie." Had she covered the slight tremor in her voice?

"Sophie?" A long pause ensued. "Oh, the tenant. Is there a problem with the cottage?" Boredom dripped from her tone.

Sophie fought back a rude retort. What a bitch. Apparently, Nick hadn't informed Heather that he was seeing her.

"No, nothing wrong with the house. Just tell him I called, please. Thanks." She hung up, the initial elation over the flowers deflating.

Maybe Nick sent flowers to all the women he slept with. If Heather, who worked with him daily, had no clue they were involved, maybe she'd read too much into last night. She shouldn't assume anything from his note or gift.

Hell, the flowers were probably a send-off gift. After sleeping with her, he was probably sprinting for the hills to escape the woman with the steamer trunk overflowing with issues. What healthy, awesome man would want to be with her?

Glancing at the clock, Sophie cursed her mother. Going to a fancy lunch held about as much appeal as a root canal. Oh well, at least it would distract her from obsessing over the Heather situation. She grabbed her keys and headed into town.

Pulling up at the Surf and Sand Hotel, she squared her shoulders and donned her invisible armor for an hour of Martine. At least she looked the part in a simple ice-blue summer sheath and strappy nude sandals, a far cry from her daily attire in the last few weeks.

Her mother waved from a table nestled by the balcony overlooking the powerful Pacific Ocean. As usual, she looked beautiful, a petite, glamorous redhead with a porcelain-doll face. In a nod to her mother's French heritage, Sophie greeted her with a kiss on each cheek.

"Ah, you look lovely, Sophie, very elegant." Her mother sounded relieved. What did she expect? That she'd show up in her pajamas?

"Thanks, Maman. What a surprise to see you. How's everything?" She settled into her chair and picked up a menu. The faster she ordered lunch, the sooner she could escape.

"I'm fine, but I'm worried about you. This impulsive tantrum has gone too far. You must move back to San Diego and get a real job. Nobody will take care of you but yourself, and you can't squander your savings while you chase pipe dreams." Her mother leaned closer, her dark eyes intent.

Sophie recoiled, shifting back in her seat. So much for being the ladies who lunch. She inhaled deeply. Exhaled a steadying breath.

"Nice to see you too. Look, I appreciate your concern, but everything's going well for me here. I'm healing. I'm independent. I'm making a life for myself." Why couldn't her mother accept her as she was?

"Ahh, I am glad you're feeling better after what happened with that bastard who humiliated you. Didn't I tell you he would cheat on you? Leave you?" Her sculpted eyebrows winged upward, a knowing expression marring her beauty.

She ground her molars together and prayed for patience. "Mother…"

Her mother's ivory complexion suffused with color as she warmed to her favorite topic: never trust any man. "I warned you. Men are all alike. Just like your pitiful excuse of a father. He ran off with some slut, left us high and dry, without a cent. You know this, and yet you got engaged to someone just like your father—a charming snake."

"Yes, you were right. Does that make you happy? But I don't remember my father, so how could I pick someone just like him? I'm getting over my mistake. I refuse to believe that all men are evil." Sophie hissed and gripped the edges of her chair.

A waiter approached, and her mother flicked him away like a pesky fly. He scuttled back, not eager to interrupt their obviously tense exchange.

"Look, I love you. I only tell you this because I want you to be happy. But you need to be practical. You're twenty-eight years old, not a child. Believing you can write a book and make enough to live is ridiculous…" Her mother threw up a slender hand.

"Enough. I didn't come here to be attacked. You're right—I'm not a child, so don't treat me like one. I've never asked you for a dime. Ever. I've worked and saved my money since I was fifteen years old. This is *my* dream. If I fail, well, that's my problem. What I won't do is live my life based on fear. So don't ever tell me again what I have to do." Tremors shook her whole body, but no way would she back down now.

Martine's lips flattened into an unattractive line. "Do you think becoming a famous novelist will bring back your fiancé? Your father? That they'll be impressed?"

"I'm done here." Sophie shoved away from the table and forced herself to put one foot in front of the other. Far away from her mother's bitterness and scorn.

Away from the past. Toward the future, whatever it might hold.

# CHAPTER 13

*N*ick glanced at his cell phone for what seemed like the hundredth time this morning. Nothing from Sophie. Once again, his preoccupation with her was interrupting his work. Damn it, she was blowing hot and cold, and he didn't have time to brood over her. He had deadlines.

Now she'd indulged in some hot rebound sex, she was done? Was the vulnerable sweet side he'd seen just a mask? Had she used him?

Not even a thank-you text for the flowers he'd hoped would make her smile. No response. Irritation simmered through him, and he glared out the window.

"Whoa, big brother. What's with the glower?"

Nick turned to face his sister, who had once again silently appeared in his office. Her brow creased and she shut the door.

"Alyssa, hey. It's nothing." Shrugging a shoulder, he cursed his temper—since when did he have a temper?

"Right, you always sit around shooting death stares while

looking off into space. Did you get bad news about this year's Pritzker Prize or something?"

Thank god she'd assumed his distress was work-related. Like he needed his sister involved in his relationship with Sophie. He hesitated––maybe Alyssa knew something he didn't.

Damn, was this what he was relegated to? A lovestruck teenager trying to see if his sister could help him win the girl? Or not win the girl if she was too broken to be in a relationship?

Hell, maybe he was simply losing his mind. "No. Just a lot going on."

"Is it a woman? Is Heather being a pain, and you need to fire her?" She waggled her eyebrows.

His lips twitched. "Enough about Heather. You know I need her."

Although yesterday he'd caught Heather checking out his ass. Why had Alyssa pointed it out to him? Life had been much simpler when Heather had been his competent manager. A professional, focusing on some other guy's ass, not his.

But the bottom line was Heather had been vital in his progress toward winning the highly coveted Pritzker Prize. Her diligence, ability to package his achievements, and connections were why he was finally in contention. He'd worked too long toward his dream to jeopardize his chances.

Alyssa tucked a strand of hair behind her ear. "So have you seen Sophie again?"

"Well, actually… Yeah, we've gone out a few times." *Even though I may have been a booty call.* Who ever thought he'd mind a hot one-night stand? Go figure.

Alyssa crossed the room and grabbed his hands. "That's awesome. Is it serious?"

"Who knows? I sent her flowers yesterday and haven't heard from her." And he sounded like a temperamental child.

"You? Flowers? Interesting... Are you sure she received them?" Her smile was smug. She knew damn well he didn't send flowers often.

"According to the flower company, yeah." Received and ignored. Radio silent.

Alyssa waved a hand. "Just call her. Don't be stubborn. You're obviously stressing about it. Life's too short."

He massaged the back of his neck. "Whatever. Do you want to grab dinner later? I'm meeting Brandt if you want to join us."

She wrinkled her nose. "Is Sophie coming too?"

"It doesn't look like it, does it?" Again, could he stop sounding like a petulant kid? Hell. He was in trouble.

"You know what, I'll swing by the cottage and see what's going on. I'll call you." Blowing him a kiss, Alyssa exited as quietly as she'd arrived.

Nick rolled his shoulders back, trudged to his desk, and snapped open the hospital file. Which he'd probably stare at blankly until he heard from Sophie or his sister.

Who was he?

# CHAPTER 14

*E*very muscle in Sophie's legs shrieked in protest as she jogged up the steep hill toward the cottage. Unable to settle her nerves after the scene with her mother, she'd attempted to clear her mind with some good old-fashioned exercise. Luckily, she hadn't passed anybody on her fast-paced trot because tears flowed down her cheeks the entire time. Despite time and distance, her mother could still push her buttons with zero effort.

Infuriating.

A bead of sweat trickled down her back, pasting her tissue-thin tank top to her skin. She welcomed the physical exhaustion, a pleasant respite from her mental and emotional turmoil. Time to return to her original vision for her new life: healing her heart and writing her book. Not necessarily in that order—ha. Although she'd blown her "year of celibacy" out the window with Nick.

She marched the rest of the way up the incline, eager to start fresh. At the tree-lined curve of the driveway, she heard the click of a car engine turning off. Maybe it was Nick? Her heart skipped a beat, and she hurried up the path.

Instead, Alyssa was parked next to her car. And Nick's sister was peering into the front window. What in the world?

Huffing out a breath, she called out, "Alyssa?"

Alyssa whirled––her eyes wide. "There you are…your car was here so I was just tapping on the window because you didn't answer the door. I thought you might hear me better from the window."

Her words were rushed. Out of character. *Huh.*

"I was out for a jog, needed to clear my head a bit." Understatement of the century.

Alyssa's smoky blue eyes narrowed. "Is everything okay?"

Sophie shrugged and avoided her gaze. "Yeah, sure, everything's fine. What's up?"

Alyssa smoothed back her long blonde hair. "I was just close by and dropped by to see if you're up for a beach walk or a glass of wine?"

"That's so sweet of you. But I need to plant myself in front of the computer for the foreseeable future. Raincheck?" No need for Nick's sister to see how red and puffy her eyes were.

"Sure but can I come in for a second and use the bathroom?"

"Of course, come on in. I'm sorry I didn't mean to be rude; I've just got a lot on my mind." Like obsessing over your brother.

The moment they walked inside, Sophie frowned. Why had she prominently displayed the magnificent bouquet right smack in the middle of the living room? Because no way could she lie to Nick's little sister about who sent them.

"Wow, how gorgeous." Alyssa made an elaborate show of sniffing the colorful assortment of flowers displayed in her favorite emerald-green vase. She smiled over her shoulder. "Who sent you these?"

Sophie nibbled on the inside of her cheek. "Well, I feel kind of awkward telling you this, but they're from Nick."

Alyssa pressed one hand to her heart. "Great. I'm so happy that you two are dating. I think you two are perfect together."

"You do?"

"Of course. Can you pretty please postpone the writing a little longer? Can we have a glass of wine, and you can spill the deets? I've been waiting for my brother to meet the right woman." Alyssa headed toward the kitchen, and Sophie trailed behind her.

"Didn't you have to use the bathroom?"

Alyssa gave a sheepish smile and headed off toward the bathroom. "Oh yeah, forgot in the excitement. Will you open some wine?"

"Well...why not. Just one glass. I do still have to write more today." She responded to Alyssa's retreating back. One glass might help free her muse, right?

Sophie poured them two glasses of her favorite French Chablis, perfect for the late-afternoon warmth. When Alyssa returned, they went outside and sat on the bench.

Alyssa leaned in and placed one hand on her arm. "I have a confession. I knew Nick sent you the flowers. I saw him earlier today, and he seemed really bummed out. I wanted to ask you if you knew why that would be?"

Her breath caught. "Bummed out? Like upset or angry?"

Alyssa shook her head. "No, more like disappointed––out of character for him. He wouldn't tell me what was bugging him."

"Well, I have no idea because I called him to thank him, and he never called me back." Her fingers gripped the stem of her wineglass. "It made me wonder if they were blow-off flowers or something."

A line formed between Alyssa's brows. "No way. I can tell he's really interested in you. Did you leave him a message?"

"Well, his office manager answered his phone and said he was in a meeting. I left a message with her."

"Heather? I can't stand her. Why didn't you call his cell?"

"I did call his cell, and she answered. Which seemed strange to me." Way too reminiscent of her ex's shady double life.

Alyssa frowned. "Oh, Nick will be pissed she answered his cell and didn't pass along your message. What is that woman playing at? I've told him to fire her so many times."

"I hate to ask, but did they ever date? She watches him like a hawk watches a rabbit." Not to mention Mallory at the grocery store mentioning she was after him.

"No, never. She's connected in the architecture industry, family ties or something. He just says she's great at her job and essential somehow to his obsession with winning the Pritzker." Alyssa paused to sip her wine.

"I have no doubt she's always perfectly charming to his face, you know, like the evil girls on *The Bachelor* who are sweet to the guy and horrible to the other girls." Alyssa sucked in her cheekbones and puffed out her lips in a fake kissy face.

Sophie laughed. "Perfect imitation. You're exactly right."

"Okay, this is ridiculous. She's obviously after my brother. He's not into her and would never cross the work line anyway. Send him a text. He's disappointed he didn't hear from you. But he'd be mortified if he knew I told you."

"Are you sure?"

Alyssa winked. "Absolutely. And one more secret: I've never known my brother to send flowers before."

Hope sparked inside her. "Okay, I'll do it. I hope you're right."

With Alyssa cheering her on, she texted Nick. He responded instantly. A few flirtatious messages later and they had dinner plans. Anticipation sparked up her spine.

"See? My work here is done." Alyssa hugged her and rose from the bench. "I've got to run."

"Thanks for coming by. Now I'll be able to focus on writing this afternoon. And who knows, maybe it was simply an oversight on Heather's part." Although her gut told her the woman knew exactly what she was doing.

"Yeah, right. Don't worry about her and have fun tonight." Alyssa snorted and sauntered back to her car.

Sophie hugged her arms around her waist and practically skipped back to the house. Time to shower, write, and be ready when Nick picked her up.

DINNER INCLUDED a few of her favorite things: wood-fired margherita pizza, Chianti, and Nick. Pushing any concerns to the back of her mind, she chose to take the evening hour by hour and savor not just the delicious food but also his charming company.

Being with Nick was easy. In the past, friends had advised her relationships should be easy, especially in the beginning, but she'd never experienced it for herself. Never truly understood until Nick. Finally, their words clicked.

Learning more about how much he loved architecture and how he'd left a big firm in Irvine to follow his heart by opening his own firm, a few years ago intrigued her. Kind of like her leaving the magazine job to follow her own dreams. He shared how he was immersed in creating a new wing for Memorial Hospital and focused on a pet project redesigning a local museum.

"The museum sounds exciting. What made you so passionate about helping them? Are you a big art lover?" She leaned closer.

He gazed down at his plate. "My mother loved art and spent hours volunteering at the museum. I want to honor her memory. And this project could turn the tides for my contention for the Pritzker Prize."

Sophie's heart stuttered and she covered his hand with hers. "I'm so sorry. How long has she been gone? And how does your father handle it?"

"They were killed in a car accident while on holiday in Ireland. Fifteen years ago." He intertwined his fingers with hers.

Her throat tightened. "That's terrible. You and Alyssa were so young. Who took care of you?"

"Me. I was in my second year at Cornell. Alyssa had just started high school, so it was especially hard on her. It all worked out." He blew out a breath.

"Oh, Nick. Didn't you have any relatives who could have helped? Raising a teenager couldn't have been easy." Her heart ached for their loss.

He shook his head, a faraway look in his emerald eyes. "Both of our parents were only children, and our grandparents had passed. It wasn't easy, but she's amazing."

"You're amazing, Nicholas Morgan." His strength blew her away. She pressed a gentle kiss on his cheek.

"Don't start kissing me again, or we'll be back at my house before dessert," he quirked a brow.

Shivers danced along her skin, but she wanted to lighten the mood and learn more about him. "Okay, tell me more about the Pritzker. You've mentioned it a few times."

"It's the most prestigious award in architecture, kind of like the Nobel Prize. My dad was nominated but passed away before he could win." His square jaw tightened. "It's my legacy."

She squeezed his hand tight. "I understand. I'm sure you'll achieve it."

His expression cleared. "Thank you. Now tell me more about this story you're writing."

"If I told you, I'd have to kill you." She smiled and shook her head. "Kidding. But there is a sexy love interest."

He flashed a wicked grin and through the rest of dinner, she basked in the sparkle in his deep green eyes and the way he never stopped touching her, brushing a strand of hair behind her ear, leaning in to kiss her between bites of pizza. Her heart blossomed under his focus. What a novelty to be the center of his attention, as if she were the only woman in the world.

When he went to the restroom, she smiled to herself, joy filling her being. She gasped and jolted upright––oh crap–– she was falling in love with Nick. *Was* in love with Nick. How had this happened so fast?

Or was she simply reacting to the attention of a gorgeous, charming, intelligent, seemingly perfect man?

Wait a second, could she picture him with her in five years? In ten? Forever?

Yes, yes, and yes. At the cottage. Traveling the world. Snuggling on the couch with Zack and Bailey. Making love. She could even visualize him with silver hair––her very own silver fox.

"Sophie?" Nick returned and slid back in next to her on the red leather booth. "You look like the cat who swallowed the cream. Care to share?"

Her smile deepened, she placed her hands on either side of his face and planted a passionate kiss on his lips. He slanted his mouth across hers, deepening the kiss. She moaned and pressed against him.

"Umm…excuse me?" a voice stammered from somewhere over Sophie's shoulder.

Nick kept her in the circle of his powerful embrace and turned toward the interruption. Sophie glanced up and the red-faced young waitress looked as if she wanted to be anywhere but in front of them.

"Can I bring you anything else?" She stared a few feet above their heads.

"Just the check, thanks." Nick turned back to her and continued the kiss where he'd left off.

Sophie had never been a PDA-type of person, but with Nick, discretion was overrated. Her body tingled, her heart raced, and heat sparked all the way down to her toes.

Time to exit the restaurant, rip his clothes off, and have her way with him.

Without releasing her, Nick smacked down a wad of cash and backed her out the front door of the restaurant all the way to his car.

Nick kept his lips fused with hers while he fumbled with the car keys, trying to get the door open. "I can't get enough of you. If it were darker in this parking lot, I would take you up against this car right now," he growled.

Sophie arched against him, rocking into the steel ridge of his arousal. Heat shot straight to her core. He made her feel powerful. Sexy. Beautiful.

And ignited her own passion. "Take me home. Drive fast."

They tumbled into the car, he sped home as she leaned over him, rained kisses along the warm skin on his throat, and stroked him through his jeans.

"Sophie, you'll kill us both if you don't stop. I can't even see straight." His hands gripped the steering wheel—knuckles white.

Her lips curved, and she slid her hand back up to his chest, savoring the feel of his thundering heartbeat.

"Hurry, hurry, hurry," she chanted.

Nick screeched to a stop in front of his house and practically dragged her out of the car. He yanked the door open, pushed her inside, and slammed the door shut. Fisting his hands in her hair, he kissed her and shoved her against the wall.

With one hand, he reached down, tugged up her skirt, and tore off her thong. He groaned when he cupped her. "You're so wet, so ready for me."

Her head fell back against the door, and he dragged his teeth along her throat. Her back bowed and she gripped his shoulders. When he thrust two thick fingers inside her and pressed his palm against her clit, her knees buckled. If he hadn't pinned her against the door, she would have slid to the floor.

"God, Nick, more. Now. I need you inside me now." Her breath came in harsh pants, and she rocked into his strong hand.

His lips curved against her mouth, and he picked up the pace. He dropped his mouth to her chest and licked her diamond-hard nipples through the thin material of her sundress. "Patience, baby. I'm going to make you come first."

She raked her nails down his back, convinced she'd lose her mind if he didn't hurry up. "Nick…please...please."

He withdrew his hand, dropped to his knees, and nudged her trembling legs apart.

"Be patient, beautiful, I have to taste you first." He gazed up at her, his eyes hooded, his grin wicked.

He licked her in one long stroke, like he was savoring a delicious dessert, then thrust his tongue inside her heat. Every muscle in her body froze when the orgasm slammed through her. He kept her thighs in a firm grip and continued his relentless assault through endless aftershocks.

He rose, trailing kisses up her slick, sweaty body, and

caught her mouth with a rough kiss. With one hand supporting her, he grabbed a condom from his back pocket, unzipped his jeans, and filled her with one powerful thrust. Somehow she mustered the strength to wrap her legs around his waist as he pounded her into the wall.

He took her in long, deep strokes and she tilted her hips to meet each and every one. Was it possible to die of pleasure?

"Sophie, again. Come with me now," he demanded, his face buried in the crook of her neck.

Who was she to refuse? A starburst of lights detonated behind her eyes down to her center and he cried out her name. They climaxed and together slid boneless to the floor.

Nick rolled onto his back, cradling her on top of him to protect her from his weight. She buried her face against his chest. They struggled to suck in oxygen, sounding like two climbers who'd reached the peak of Mt. Whitney.

When they'd caught their breath, he swooped her up in his arms, carried her into the bedroom, and deposited her on the enormous bed. He stood and shucked his clothes—he'd been fully dressed and for some reason, his impatience to be inside her turned her on even more.

They scooted under the covers, still not talking, still blown away by their ferocious lovemaking.

Nick stroked a damp strand of hair away from her forehead. His eyes darkened as he stared down at her, his expression suddenly serious. "You are the most amazing woman I've ever met. I've never felt like this before. I meant to take it slow…"

Her breath hitched. "Kiss me again." She tugged his leonine head down to meet her lips. With a groan, he swirled and stroked his tongue with hers.

A while later, he pulled Sophie close, spooning her back to his front. Connected and warm, her mind raced, and nerves skittered down her spine. She wasn't ready to confess her feelings to him yet. It was way too soon to tell him she loved him. Her heart couldn't handle another rejection.

Because what if everything between them was only mind-blowing chemistry?

## CHAPTER 15

*N*ick drifted awake, his muscles relaxed, his mind calm. He propped himself up on one elbow and gazed down at Sophie, who continued to doze, her dark fringe of lashes resting on her porcelain skin. They fit together perfectly, like puzzle pieces. Even asleep, in the early morning light, she was the most beautiful woman he'd ever seen. His chest tightened, full of unaccustomed feelings of possessiveness and protectiveness.

Was this love? As if he would battle anyone or anything to keep her safe. He hadn't realized anything was missing from his life. In fact, his life was pretty damn good. But now everything seemed more vibrant for one simple reason--Sophie.

No woman had pulled him in like Sophie. A memory flashed of when his father shared that the moment he'd set eyes on his mother, he'd known she was the one. Married after a mere three months, they'd been the perfect couple.

Was it the Morgan way? Fall once. Fall forever.

Nick's parents would have loved Sophie. They would've been thrilled for him to find what they'd shared. And they would have encouraged him not to waste a moment. If she was the one, no reason existed to delay starting their life together. Why wait?

She stirred and arched her back, pressing her perfect ass up against his morning wood. He leaned down and grazed the sensitive spot he'd discovered on her neck and was rewarded by the eruption of goosebumps along her soft skin. When she turned her head, her eyes still closed, he captured her tempting pink mouth.

Everything suddenly seemed crystal clear.

Her big blue eyes opened, and her lips curved upward. "What are you staring at, handsome?"

He turned her to face him and cupped her cheek. *What the hell, here goes nothing.*

"Sophie, this isn't how I planned to tell you this, but I can't wait." Sweat prickled on the back of his neck. "I'm in love with you."

She gasped and a huge smile spread across her face. She caught his wrist with one hand. "Nick, I love you too. I know this is crazy fast, but I love you."

Happiness coursed through him, and he rained kisses on her forehead, her cheeks, and her nose, before wrapping his arms around her and pulling her in tight.

Sophie loved him too. Nothing had ever felt this good. Nothing.

"You've made me the happiest man alive. I've never said those words before. Never felt them. They're all for you, my love."

Sophie hugged him closer, her hands stroking along his back and every muscle in his body leaped to attention.

This time, he forced himself to go slow and cherish every luscious inch of her. He'd never get enough of her. The little sounds she made in the back of her throat, the feel of being buried inside her tight hot center, the knowledge she loved

111

him too, drove him wild. Circling her sensitive bud with his thumb, he slid one then two fingers inside her. She was ready for him. He made her explode with his fingers before allowing himself to slide into her heat. She wrapped around him like a hot, tight fist, and he couldn't hold back a deep groan. They made sweet, slow love—like a fantasy come alive. Once she started to come apart in his arms, he let go and they went tumbling over the edge together.

After a few moments, he lifted his head, gazed down at her, and repeated his earlier declaration. "I love you. You're mine now."

Her eyes sparkling, she lifted one hand to his jaw and whispered, "I'm yours and you're mine. And we need a shower."

His lips twitched. Yeah, they'd gotten sweaty and messy––and sexy as hell.

They rose, went into the bathroom, and Sophie turned on the shower, the heat immediately steaming up the room. They stepped into the shower together.

"You are so gorgeous." He poured body wash into his hands and soaped her breasts, down her belly, to her hot core. She arched into his hand, and he stroked her––he couldn't get enough of this woman. *His* woman.

"But it's my turn to clean you up." Without looking away, she rubbed some bath gel between her palms, then stroked down his chest and abs until she wrapped her fingers around him. His cock sprang to attention.

He groaned and dropped his head back. "Baby, that feels so good."

"I think you need a little more." She dropped to her knees and keeping one hand wrapped around his base, slowly took him into her mouth.

He hissed and wrapped his hands in her hair. "Sophie…"

She hummed around him, and heat curled down his

spine. The sight of her on her knees, the feel of her perfect mouth and talented tongue stroking him almost made him detonate on the spot. She was driving him wild. He couldn't wait another second.

He retreated a step, and she gazed up at him. "Baby, I need to be inside you right now or I'll lose it. But we don't have a condom."

"I'm on the pill. It's fine."

He grabbed her thighs and in one swift move, lifted her, and thrust inside of her, pressing her back into the shower wall. It wouldn't be sleepy and quiet this time. Her fingernails dug into his back as she took him inside her.

All of him.

"Faster, Nick. Deeper." She slid her hands down to his ass and gripped him hard.

He roared and pounded into her, unable to slow down if he tried. Urgent strokes, murmured encouragement, complete abandonment. She began pulsing around him and he couldn't hold out.

"Nick, I'm coming. Oh my god."

"Sophie." He groaned, dropped his head against the wall and came hard.

Sophie blinked, struggling to focus as she gazed into his eyes. He recognized the awe she was feeling because he, too, was simply blown away. His chest tightened as she smiled up at him.

Amazing.

Her blue eyes swept downward. He'd loved how uninhibited, how passionate, how responsive she'd been. She was his. He wanted to beat his chest with his fists and yell it out to the four corners of the earth.

"Can I make us some breakfast?" She smiled up at him through her thick fringe of black lashes.

He squeezed her perfect ass one more time and leaned into her, savoring the way she fit against him.

Gazing deep into her eyes, he replied, "I. Would. Love. Breakfast. With. You. Beautiful."

"I'm going to need something to put on?"

He stepped out of the shower and grabbed two towels for them. He tugged on a pair of worn-in sweats and grabbed one of his T-shirts from the folded pile of laundry sitting on his teakwood dresser.

She tugged the T-shirt over her head, and it reached midthigh, emphasizing her long, shapely dancer's legs. "Mmm, it smells like you."

"You like that?" Nick's mouth watered at how sexy she looked. He'd never view his T-shirt the same way again.

"Umm, you know I love the way you smell." Her high cheekbones were flushed, her lips swollen and pink. "So, where's the kitchen? I'm starving."

"Me too. Come with me, gorgeous." He caught her hand and led the way.

# CHAPTER 16

*E*xcitement coursed through Sophie's veins––they'd been so lucky to find each other. It was real. They loved each other. Totally unexpected but totally perfect. Her hand tingled where it was connected with his and it was all she could do not to skip down the spacious hallway.

Because they'd been wrapped up in each other last night, she hadn't noticed the décor, so she checked out Nick's house while they traversed the spacious hallway. The ceilings were high, and large windows dominated the rooms. Pearl-gray walls, deep teakwood accents, and beams on the living room ceiling led into the open kitchen. With sleek modern architecture, but with warmth and a sense of comfort––the house was incredible.

They headed to the gigantic stainless-steel refrigerator and Nick pulled out eggs, spinach, cheese, and bread along with a bottle of orange juice. Sophie began brewing a strong pot of coffee and hummed *Madness*, her favorite Muse song.

"Do you want to have a seat at the breakfast bar, or do you want to watch from afar while I whip us up something yummy?"

Nick leaned in for another kiss. "How about I watch from right here?"

Heat curled down her spine and she pressed one hand against his bare, solid chest. "You can watch from wherever you want but could you pour me a cup of coffee with a splash of milk? I'll I get our omelet started?"

"Yeah, it wasn't like you let me get much sleep last night?" He winked.

She laughed. "Umm, are you complaining?"

"Definitely not complaining."

She admired the way his broad shoulders tapered down to a lean waist and perfect butt. When she accepted her coffee mug from him, it took all her willpower not to step in for another kiss. They needed sustenance.

While she whipped up a Greek omelet, they drank their coffee in companionable silence. The wheat toast popped out of the toaster just as she slid the omelet onto two plates.

"It's perfect outside. Let's take our breakfast to the patio, okay?" he said and picked up both plates.

She followed him out to an enormous patio, with panoramic views of the Pacific and all the lush greenery for which Laguna Beach was famous.

Sophie sighed in contentment and savored the sunshine warming her skin. Completely comfortable wearing his T-shirt, despite her hair likely looking as if a family of rats had taken up residence, happiness filled her.

All because of Nick. The four incredible lovemaking sessions and the orgasms she'd stopped counting didn't hurt. Nick loved her. And she would savor every minute, for however long it lasted. Life was short, and she wouldn't let her past and her hasty vow of celibacy prevent her from seeing where this went with him.

Now that they'd made love, she couldn't imagine denying

herself the pleasure he could give her. That they gave to each other.

"This is the best omelet I've ever tasted. I didn't know you could cook too."

Her lips twitched. "Well, don't get too excited. This is one of about five things that I can make. I'm not much of a cook at all."

"Does that mean I get to have four more meals with you wearing just my T-shirt?" He clasped her chin in one strong hand and nibbled on her lower lip.

Heat rose in her cheeks. How could a comment like that make her blush when she'd been screaming like a wild woman for half of the night? Maybe the light of morning made her feel a little more reserved and a bit embarrassed at her unbridled enthusiasm. But Nick seemed happy and carefree too, so she'd roll with it.

He framed her face in both hands and deepened the kiss. "Or we could head back into the shower?"

Her breath caught in her throat. "You are kidding, right? I'm not going to be able to walk tomorrow."

His brow furrowed. "Did I hurt you?"

She shook her head. "No, no, I'm fine, but your stamina is over the top."

"It's you, Sophie. But I do need to head into the office, so another shower will have to wait. Let's go back inside." His voice grew husky.

Her heart clutched. "There's something I should tell you," she began as she followed him inside.

He gazed back at her. "I don't like the sound of that."

"No, no more deep dark secrets. It's about your office manager."

He quirked a tawny brow—a gesture she was beginning to recognize. "Heather?"

"Well, I wanted to tell you why you hadn't heard from me

earlier when I received the flowers. Thank you again, by the way."

He leaned back against the counter and gestured for her to continue with one hand.

"So, I did call you right after I received the flowers because I was excited."

Nick's lips flattened into a tight line. "When? I didn't get a call or message."

She smoothed her tangled hair back from her face. "Well, that's the thing. I called you right after I opened the card, and Heather answered the phone. She said she'd tell you I called. And then I never heard back from you, so I was bummed."

Nick's scowl deepened. "What? You called me at the office? Why didn't you call my cell?"

"That's the thing. I did call your cell."

He smacked his coffee cup onto the counter. "What? What is she doing answering my cell phone? She never told me. She better have a good explanation."

*Good.* "I thought it was strange and didn't know if they were blow-off flowers. If Alyssa hadn't come over, I wouldn't have figured it out." One more confirmation that his office manager's feelings were one-sided. Maybe he'd fire the plastic-face, store-bought-boob snake.

His nostrils flared and his jaw tightened."Forgetting to deliver a message is one thing, but answering my private cell is just unacceptable. I'm glad my sister told you."

Nick crossed the kitchen in two strides, pulled her into his arms, and slanted his mouth against hers. After a few satisfying minutes, he stepped back.

"Well, that won't happen again. Speaking of work, I really need to get into the office. But you can take all the time you need. Just lock the door behind you."

She bit her lip. "Umm…this sounds awful, but where are

we? I don't have my car and didn't…umm…pay attention on the ride back to your house last night."

Nick grinned. "Yeah, that was quite a ride. We're just up the hill from the cottage, on the other side of the grove of trees."

"What? I'm living on the same piece of property as you? I had no idea."

"Convenient, right? I can give you a ride down if you're ready or again feel free to take your time and walk back." He winked. "I wish I had some more time because I have some plans for you, beautiful."

Nerves bubbled in her throat. Did she want to live right down the hill from him? What happened if it ended? Swallowing her trepidation, Sophie forced a laugh. "What makes you think I don't have plans for you too?"

"I wouldn't have it any other way. Can I see you tonight? Dinner?"

She stepped in again for a last kiss. "I'd love that."

"I love you. I've got to get ready." He stroked her cheek.

"I love you, too." Thrilled to say it and mean it, no matter how fast it had happened.

He headed out the door, and she sank onto a barstool, wrapping her arms tightly around her waist. How had her life changed so much in a few short weeks? Could she trust these feelings? Could she trust him? She hadn't been looking for love.

They'd declared their love for each other. After less than a month

Crap, she'd promised herself not to get involved. That once she'd healed her heart, she'd meet a guy, take it slow, be friends with him first, and wait to take things to a physical level. Way to stick to her wonderful post-breakup plan. Ha ha—talk about shooting down her not-dating-for-a-year plan down in flames.

Nicholas Morgan's dog had knocked her flat on her back. And Nick hadn't been far behind Bailey in sweeping her off her feet. Her gut told her he was sincere.

Despite her mother's dire predictions.

But Nick was handsome and charming and moving really fast. Doug had been the same way in the beginning. Dazzling her with his charm and charisma. Was she repeating a pattern?

Damn these doubts tugging at her gut. She'd resolved to live in the present moment, to grab joy with both hands when it was presented to her.

Alyssa's approval and excitement about them being a couple meant a lot. Come to think of it, Kelly had adored him too. Her best friend had hated Doug from day one, and she'd been correct. Interesting. Same with her cat––hissed at Doug and purred for Nick.

No, she wasn't the same woman she'd been when she fell for Doug. Now she knew what she wanted, and she'd been direct with Nick. She'd trust her gut and heart.

Love.

She sighed, pressing her hand to her heart. After all, although her novel was chick lit, romance was at its heart and the love story between the two main characters.

She believed in happily ever after, and damn it, maybe this was her chance.

# CHAPTER 17

*N*ick spent the short drive to his office grinding his molars and drumming his fingers on the steering wheel. He ran through what he'd learned about his office manager again and struggled to reconcile Heather's recent behavior with the ultra-professional person who'd helped him so much with his business. Although his sister had warned him that Heather had designs on him, he'd simply never looked at the woman that way.

Which didn't exactly make him feel comfortable. But as far as he knew, Heather didn't know about his personal involvement with Sophie, so why the hell would she not pass along the message? Beyond the inappropriateness of her answering his cell phone, to do it and then neglect to tell him Sophie had called? He blew out a steadying exhale. He'd straighten out this drama straightaway.

When he entered the office, the lobby was deserted, and Heather's door was closed. Without bothering to knock, he barked out her name.

She opened her door, her eyes wide. "Good morning, Nick. Is everything okay?"

"No, everything is not okay. Come into my office and sit down. We need to talk." He kept his tone neutral as he strode into his office without a backward glance.

"Nick?" She hurried in and sat down. "Did something happen with the hospital contract?"

"No." He narrowed his eyes. "How many times have you answered my cell phone?"

"Umm, what do you mean?" She gazed down at her fake fingernails.

"The question is straightforward. I'll repeat it for you. Have you been answering my cell when I'm not around?"

She shrugged a shoulder and gazed at him, the picture of confused innocence. "Well…a few times. We'd been waiting on a status update for the Pritzker application, and I didn't want us to miss out on anything."

*Was she kidding with this?* "A few times? How many? Who called?"

She tapped her fingers against her lips. "Let me think. Maybe just once or twice? Luckily, it wasn't anyone important, so I didn't mention it."

"Nobody important? And who are you to decide?" Annoyance rolled through him. How the hell had he missed her evasiveness? What else had she lied about?

"Oh, okay, now I remember." She gestured with one hand. "Your tenant called the other day. Ms. Barnes? She said there wasn't a problem at the cottage. It must have slipped my mind."

"I've never known anything to slip your mind before. But now I don't know if you've been hiding other things from me." Hell would have frozen over at the frost in his tone. "You had no right to answer my cell phone, and if you do it again or I discover any other things you've been doing here behind my back, I'm going to have to let you go."

The color drained from her cheeks, and she pressed one

hand to her throat. "I'm so sorry and of course, I'm not hiding things from you. I was in your office looking for some plans, and it was instinct. Don't you think firing me is a little extreme?"

"No, I don't. You know I value honesty and privacy above everything. Is there anything else you need to share with me?" There damn well better not be.

She shook her head. "Nick, you know I only want what's best for you and your firm. I didn't intend to upset you. Please accept my apology." She glanced down at her clasped hands, but not before he caught a glimpse of her expression, which looked like she'd sucked on a lemon.

Perhaps his sister's instincts were correct about Heather. How had he missed it before? What else was she hiding underneath her perfect office manager façade?

"Okay, but if anything out of line happens again, you'll be packing up your office. And if Sophie Barnes calls on my office phone, you page me immediately. Are we clear?" Because he called bullshit on her "forgetting" to pass along Sophie's message.

In the eighteen months Heather had worked for him, she'd been conscientious and forthright. But he had to trust whoever worked for him and Heather's behavior was odd, at best. Was she purposefully deceiving him? And had she done it before?

"Nick…"

"You can go." He shuffled the papers on his desk and didn't look up.

Without another word, Heather exited, closing the door softly behind her. He massaged the tight cords on the back of his neck. Shit, what a mess--he couldn't lose the Pritzker now. Not after dedicating his life's work to attaining his dream.

# CHAPTER 18

*S*ophie stretched her arms overhead, then opened her email for a quick break before diving into another round of writing sprints. A message from Elizabeth, her former boss at *Healthy Woman*, popped up first. *Odd.* She'd received her final paycheck, transferred her insurance, and wasn't planning on writing any freelance articles for the foreseeable future.

She scanned the message and did a double-take. Elizabeth wanted Sophie to return to San Diego and take over the editor-in-chief position because she was considering moving out of state.

Not a chance. Not a chance in hell. At one point, Sophie had craved the masthead position. No longer. Sophie grabbed her phone and called her former boss's direct line.

Elizabeth answered on the first ring. "Sophie. Tell me you're going to be my replacement so I can feel good about leaving."

"Hi Elizabeth, slow down. I'm flattered but I'm committed to writing my book So, no, I'm not going to take your job, I'm sorry."

"Oh shoot, I thought you might be bored and eager to return to the business world. You're such a great editor and such a people person. Everyone misses you here."

"Thanks for saying that. I do miss you guys, but I love writing." Funny, Elizabeth hadn't been so complimentary when she'd been her boss.

"Aren't you worried about finances now that you're on your own? Why not write on the side and if you get published, then consider quitting."

Sophie blew out a breath. "I appreciate your concern. If at the end of this year I haven't accomplished what I want, I'll reconsider then." *And thanks for the lovely vote of confidence with the "if" instead of "when."*

"I'm sorry, I didn't mean that to come out so harshly. The job opportunity won't be here then—the time is now. I respect your decision, but you can't blame me for trying to win you back." Elizabeth's tone cooled.

Was she reckless to turn this down? "Thanks, I appreciate your confidence."

"Okay, fine, but I think you're making a mistake." Elizabeth paused. "But there's something else I need to tell you. Your ex came by here a few weeks back demanding that I give him your new address. Of course, I didn't. I was shocked to see him after everything that happened. Have you heard from him?"

Her fingers tightened on the phone and her gut churned picturing her ex barging into her former workplace. Hadn't he humiliated her enough? Elizabeth, like everyone else in her life, was aware of Doug's infidelity and the wedding-that-never-was.

"Well, he did call me the other day from a blocked number. I shouldn't have to change my phone number I've had for years because he suddenly wants to play nice." *The jerk.*

Elizabeth gasped. "He sure has nerve. What did he want?"

She snorted. "Astoundingly enough, he asked to see me to discuss getting back together. Can you believe that?"

"Seriously? After cheating on you and ditching you on your wedding day? I hope you told him to go to hell." Elizabeth's outrage carried over the phone.

"Something like that. I just want to forget him. If he comes around again, I'd really appreciate it if you don't share anything about me with him."

"Of course not. Well, if you change your mind about coming back to the magazine in any capacity, please call me. I'll let you know who ends up filling my role so you're still in the loop. Good luck and take care of yourself."

Sophie hung up and paced to the large picture window and stared out at the cloudless blue sky. No way would she allow the mention of Doug to affect her mood. But today, her emotions ran more toward anger than hurt. The man had demonstrated his true colors and he couldn't hurt her again. Elizabeth's offer was a surprise, though.

She'd focus on the positive––she'd resisted even considering returning to the sure-thing career position. If she caved at the first traditional job opportunity, she'd become one of the "if only" people. If only I hadn't had to work full-time, I'd have written a book, if only I'd had time...fill in the blank. No way.

Because when she planted her butt in the chair and filtered out the rest of the world, the words flowed amazingly well. She twirled to the couch and pressed a kiss on Zack's silky head. "You believe in me, don't you Zack? And you love having me around more, right?"

Zack blinked slowly, then rested his head on his paws and dozed off again. The universal signal for her to get back to work.

Her phone buzzed with an unknown number. A chill danced down her spine: What if it was Doug again?

Damn it, she wasn't going to live her life in fear of Doug's harassment. If it was him, she'd make it clear she never wanted to hear from him again.

"May I please speak with Sophie Barnes?" an unfamiliar woman's voice asked.

Her shoulders softened. "This is Sophie."

"Hi, it's Melissa Martin, from college. You e-mailed me last week?"

Her lips curved up. "Hi. So great to hear from you." Her former classmate was now a literary agent in New York. She'd e-mailed her for advice about getting published.

"You too. You always said you were going to write a book. Good for you. Is the manuscript finished?"

Sophie rolled her eyes. "Uh, no. But the writing is going well, and I want to be prepared when it's time to query."

"Well, for fiction, your book must be complete before you contact agents. I can send you a few websites where you can research the best agencies for you. Unfortunately, my firm focuses on non-fiction, or I'd be happy to read yours when it's ready."

Disappointment filled her. But having an old friend buy her book would be too easy, right?

"I'll send over some resources for you and I'm happy to critique your query letter, but can I be honest with you?" Melissa cleared her throat. "Don't take this the wrong way but do you have any idea how competitive the market is? Last year, I received thirty thousand query letters and only took on four new clients. It's cutthroat."

Sophie swallowed hard. *Four* out of thirty thousand? Those numbers sounded like the odds of winning the lottery. Not the statistics she needed to hear.

Melissa's discouraging tone echoed Elizabeth, her

mother, her coworkers, and even Kelly's questioning of the wisdom of quitting her job before she'd written her book.

She straightened her spine. "Well, I was at a crossroads and had some money saved. So I figured I'd put all my effort into writing this first book without the distractions of my full-time gig."

"I understand, and I'm not trying to dissuade you, but if I were you, it might be a good idea to try to get your job back if you can. I mean, even if you get an agent straightaway, it takes time to prepare and sell the book, then usually at least a year before it's published. With the economy being so tough, I hate to think of you unemployed and unpublished."

Sophie pinched the bridge of her nose and sank onto the couch. "I appreciate your opinion. I'm still set on my path for now. I'll send you an e-mail when I've finished and have a query together. Thanks again."

Damn, damn, damn. Zack leaped up into her lap and butted his head against her hand. She cuddled him in close and huffed out a disappointed breath.

In a perfect world, Melissa would've asked for her query or a few chapters, called her back, and immediately offered her a six-figure contract, including film rights. Ah, the fantasy world. But the next person who advised her to return to her day job would get an earful.

Hell, she'd questioned herself since she was a child. Vague memories of her father's leaving them and her mother's subsequent despair. Somehow, she'd taken it upon herself to be the perfect child—straight A's, captain of cheerleading, excellent college, all of it. None of her accomplishments appeased her mother's critical nature nor brought her father back.

No more. Maybe her move had been impulsive, but she was committed. If it didn't work out, she could always get another job. She'd live up to her own expectations. Follow her own dreams. Stop trying to please her mother, her boss, or anyone else for that matter.

She was a writer. Damn it. She would write her book. And now she would finish her word count goals for the day. And then she would celebrate her decision to stick to her plan and pursue her dreams. If she failed, it wouldn't be for lack of effort.

Two hours and nine-hundred words later, Sophie shut her laptop. Time to celebrate achieving her daily goals. Who better to celebrate with than Nick? She'd surprise him at the office.

After a quick shower and change into dark skinny jeans, faux-snakeskin flats, and a striped slouchy T-shirt, she was ready to go. She googled his firm's address. On impulse, she grabbed the bottle of Cristal champagne she'd been saving for a special day and headed into the village of Laguna Beach.

Driving down the winding roads into town, she sang along to the radio, enjoying the hairpin turns and verdant green foliage framing the streets. A far cry from her white-knuckle experience a few short weeks ago.

She parked in front of the standalone building with strong, simple lines, with the Morgan Designs sign over the entrance. When she opened the door, the small foyer appeared deserted. It was a beautiful space—imagine that for an architect—with tons of windows and natural light, modern and spare furniture, and some gorgeous bamboo accents.

Shoot, maybe she should have called first. His car hadn't been parked out front.

"Nick are you here?" she called toward the closed office doors.

The door to the left of the reception area opened, and Heather appeared, once again dressed like a runway model. *Marvelous.*

"Nick isn't in the office right now. Did you have an appointment?" A sneer marred what should have been an objectively attractive face.

Why was the woman such a hostile witch? Sophie gritted her teeth––time to clear the air.

She lifted her chin and glared at Heather. "I don't need an appointment to see Nick. Where is he?"

She barked out a laugh. "You consider renting his cottage to be a personal relationship? Hardly. If it were so personal, you would have known that he wasn't in the office and wouldn't show up like a desperate teenager in the throes of puppy love."

For a moment she was stunned into silence, then anger simmered through her. Was Heather kidding with this?

"Wow, your professionalism knows no bounds, does it? First answering Nick's cell phone and failing to give him a message from me and now talking to me this way? From where I'm standing, you're the employee so you should act like it." Her hands were trembling but damn if she'd let Heather see that. She turned to leave before her bravado fled.

"Oh, you're going to run crying to Nick again? Just remember he needs me. I could make one phone call, and he'd be out of contention for the Pritzker. My job is secure."

Sophie's fingers curled into fists. "Have a nice day." She turned on her heel and strode to the exit, determined not to allow this woman to see how upset she was.

Heather called out, "You are aware of his nickname, right? You're just one more bimbo in a long line for him. He'll be bored of you soon, and I'll be the one waiting."

The door slammed. Sophie sucked in an unsteady breath, pressing her hand to her churning stomach, and hurried to her car. Despite maintaining her composure in front of Heather, she was shaken. And her barbs hit home.

Nick did have a reputation as the Player of Laguna. He'd admitted he'd never been in a serious relationship. She'd hopped into bed with Nick before she knew his middle name. Still didn't know his middle name, come to think of it.

Sure he said he loved her, but it had only been a matter of weeks. Doug had been wonderful in the beginning too. And look how that had turned out. Maybe Heather was the Universe's way of reminding her to slow down. Just like Doug's betrayal had been a sign to change her life.

Bile rose in her throat as she flicked on her car's engine. The light faded from the once vivid afternoon. The confrontation with Heather plunged her back into the space from a few months ago when she'd questioned everything about her judgment.

She gripped the steering wheel and blinked the moisture gathering in her eyes.

No way could she survive going down this road again. Time to retreat.

# CHAPTER 19

Sophie poured her second glass of Cristal with Zack snuggled in her lap. The most expensive champagne she'd ever bought worked to drown her sorrows just as well as to celebrate. Maybe she was on the fast track to becoming the Crazy Old Cat Lady––the Crazy Old Champagne Drinking Cat Lady––and so what if she was?

After a lengthy phone monologue bringing her best friend up to date, she was ready to listen. She switched her phone to speaker mode and Kelly's voice filled the living room.

"Okay, I wish I was there to share that champagne with you. I think you should ignore Heather––she's clearly trying to sabotage you. I'm proud of you for turning down the job, I'm sorry about the stats on landing an agent, but I'm thrilled about you and Nick. The chemistry between you two was crackling and he really seems like a good guy."

Sophie's shoulders relaxed and her lips curved up. "Thanks, Kel. That means a lot coming from you."

"I'm always right, remember? Nick's a big boy and can

handle his career dreams just fine. Heather couldn't be that petty as to mess up such a major business deal."

"Hmm…" Her gut wasn't so sure about Heather's intentions.

"Okay, as your best friend, there are a few things I need to say. Is that cool?"

"Of course. You can tell me anything." She tipped a little more bubbly into her champagne flute—liquid courage.

"Well, here goes. I think this huge life change has been percolating since you were a little girl—way back to when your dad bailed. Your mom's done the best she can, but I think she's bitter, and I think her efforts to protect you went too far.

"You've always put on a brave face like everything is fine, but I know you. And I remember. The external milestones your mom valued above all else are bullshit. You don't need to publish a book or look a certain way or always be on your best behavior to deserve love. What happened with Doug is his fault, not yours. You don't have to prove to anyone that you are good enough. Know that you simply are."

Sophie's eyes filled. "I appreciate your honesty. My mom even said something similar when I saw her—not in a nice way—that becoming a published author wouldn't make Doug love me or my dad return. I know that. All those years of therapy have helped with my abandonment issues from my dad. Mostly."

In the last few months, she'd realized she'd stayed with Doug because of her abandonment issues from her father's desertion and her mom's conditional love. As if she'd been the perfect woman, Doug would have loved her forever. Not so much.

"I'm serious. You. Are. Good. Enough. Exactly. As. You. Are." Kelly punctuated each word.

Sophie gazed out the picture window. "Okay, okay. But

this book means so much to me. It's symbolic. I need to prove to myself I'm brave enough to follow my dreams, despite what anybody thinks."

"You are following your dreams. You are doing it, as we speak. I have faith in you, and it sounds like Nick does too."

"But it's all so new. He just seems too good to be true. You know?" That was the question, was he?

"Maybe. But your gut tells you to trust him, right?"

She pressed one hand to her belly. "Yeah, it does, but poor Nick––I don't just have a little baggage, I'm a full set of luggage."

"We all have baggage. You know I do too. But I have a great feeling about Nick. Just slow the pace down and set boundaries. But enjoy it. You deserve a knight in shining armor. You *are* worthy of love. Remember you can have it all. Ignore that spiteful bitch and let Nick deal with her."

She tucked her legs beneath her and sank further into the plush couch. "You're right. She definitely caught me off guard––I've seriously never had someone be so rude and nasty to me and you know I hate confrontation. She makes my mom's attacks look like child's play. I hope she wasn't serious about the Pritzker—it'd kill him to lose his dream."

Kelly snorted. "Your mom's all bark and no bite. She loves you, but she's got her own issues. Not your problem. I think you're on the right path with everything. Anyway, you really should share with Nick about your family. Call him and invite him to help you finish the Cristal."

They hung up, and Sophie called Nick right away, before she lost her nerve. Kelly's pep talk bolstered her sagging confidence. Hell, she should pay her best friend for a therapy session. She'd tuck her worries about Heather away for now.

"Hi Beautiful. Miss me?" His voice was gravelly and low. Sexy.

Sophie's heart took a long slow dive in her chest. "I'm sorry, did I dial the wrong number? Who is this?"

"Very funny. I was just going to call you. How about I bring over dinner and a bottle of wine? Want to watch TV with me and neck?"

A giggle bubbled up in her throat. "Necking? That sounds old-fashioned and perfect. Absolutely. I've already popped some champagne so hurry over."

"Champagne without me? I'm at Whole Foods now and I'll grab us a meal deal and be over in fifteen."

Kelly was right. She'd accept Nick at face value. No more self-doubt. Time to enjoy her independence, focus on her writing and relish this lovely surprise of a relationship. And time to toss her ratty sweats in the hamper and pull on some lacy lingerie and her "nice" yoga pants. She smoothed her hair away from her face and rose from the couch.

When he arrived, she skipped to open the door. She leaped into his arms, wrapped her legs around his waist, and planted a huge kiss on his mouth.

Laughing, Nick slid his hands to her butt and squeezed. "Now that's what I call a greeting."

"Only for you, handsome." Her heart rate kicked up when his gorgeous green eyes crinkled at the corners.

Nick set her onto her feet and turned to pick up the grocery bags from the porch. Bailey bounded into the house and headed straight for Zack. Watching the dog and cat interact warmed Sophie's heart. The animals adored each other. And her cat also perked up whenever Nick arrived. Animals knew.

As the crazy old cat lady in training, she should have trusted her cat's instincts.

As they set up dinner in the kitchen, Nick asked, "So give me the champagne-worthy news."

Her hand tightened around her fork. *Crap*, she needed to

tell him about her latest confrontation with Heather. Damn the woman for putting her in the position to feel like a tattletale, but Nick deserved to know what was happening behind his back. Maybe he could shed some light on the situation.

She exhaled a fortifying breath. "Well, I stopped by the office this afternoon with the champagne to surprise you, but you weren't there…"

"When?" His eyebrows drew together. "I only ran out to grab some lunch."

"Around one thirty, I think. When I went inside, Heather was there, and––"

Nick's jaw tightened. "What did she do this time?"

Sophie glanced down and poured Nick some champagne. "Well, she was really rude. I don't like to talk behind people's backs, but she was threatening and nasty, and I don't appreciate being treated like that."

"Threatening? What the hell is going on with her? What did she say?" His face was carved from granite, his eyes chips of ice.

She shared the high points of Heather's tirade, doing her best to keep emotion out of it. Although annoyance flared down her spine remembering just what a jerk the woman was.

"I'm going to fire her tomorrow." Nick covered the distance between them in two strides.

His strong arms wrapped around her, and his lips brushed the top of her hair. She burrowed her face into the warm skin of his neck and sighed in pleasure. He felt like home. Nobody had ever made her feel so protected. Ever.

She pressed one hand against his hard chest and gazed up at him. "Fire her? What reason will you give her? What if she sues you for wrongful termination or something? Or tries to sabotage your Pritzker nomination?" Crap, what if Heather did sabotage him? Wouldn't he eventually resent her for being in the middle of it all?

Nick hesitated for a moment and shook his head. "I won't tolerate anybody treating you that way, especially someone that works for me. Screw the Pritzker."

"You don't mean that. Think this through. You've worked for years to earn that prize. To honor your dad's memory." Sophie stroked her hands down his arms.

"I'm the architect, for god's sake. The prize is based on my life's work. Sure, she helped me put together the package in a way that's garnered me notice, but in the end, her connections to the committee shouldn't be a factor."

Was he trying to convince her or himself? "Are you sure? All I'm saying is don't do anything rash."

"You're a sweetheart. I'll make sure to check with my lawyer, but wrongful termination suits don't go far in California unless there's discrimination. I already talked to her about answering my phone and not giving me your message. I don't need to deal with this. I can let her go for not doing a satisfactory job, and her treatment of you sure as hell isn't going unpunished."

Guilt nipped at her. "Maybe just give her a warning and if she acts like this again, then consider firing her? Give her thirty days or something?

"I just know of this woman who got fired at *Healthy Woman*, my old magazine, and she made life a nightmare for my boss for over a year with her frivolous sexual harassment lawsuit. Even though it got dismissed, she cost the company a lot of money and time. Went to the press. I'd hate for Heather to pull something like that because she sure seems like she has a vengeful streak."

"Huh. I just want to throw her out on her ass for talking to you that way. You're more important to me. I'll check with my lawyer. Don't worry." His expression didn't soften.

Sophie wrapped her arms around his neck. "I'm sorry about all of it. Let's put her out of our minds. We don't want to waste this yummy Cristal."

Nick exhaled a deep breath and lifted his glass. "Well, are you going to tell me what we're toasting to? One of the big New York publishers called with a book deal?"

"Ha--I wish. So here's the good news. It isn't that big of a deal, but my former magazine offered me the editor-in-chief position."

"What? You're moving back to San Diego?" He scowled.

She grinned up at him. "No, silly. We're celebrating because I turned it down. I'm building my life here now. I'm sticking with writing my book. I'm proud of myself for staying true to my dream."

"You scared me. I thought you were excited about leaving." He tapped his glass with hers and they both drank.

Then Nick clasped her face between his hands, his eyes gleaming. "I love you so much, Sophie, and I'm the luckiest guy in the world to be with you."

She caught his hand and tugged him toward the bedroom. "Let's celebrate. Forget dinner for now. Grab the rest of that champagne...I've got some ideas."

"Whatever my soon-to-be *New York Times* bestselling author girlfriend wants." Nick snagged the bottle and followed her.

*New York Times* bestseller had a fabulous ring to it. Today had been a rollercoaster but with Nick, she felt exhilarated for the ride.

# CHAPTER 20

*I*n the morning, Nick smiled at the empty champagne bottle sitting on the nightstand. He'd never drink champagne again without reminiscing about sipping it from Sophie's smooth belly. He stroked one hand along her skin––it was sticky from the alcohol––it would be rude of him not to clean off the last few drops for her. She arched into his hand, her lips curving up.

He shifted and scooped her up in his arms and carried her to the bathroom. She giggled and wound her arms around his neck. He flipped on the shower and walked them inside. He released her and she squealed at the not-yet-hot water.

"Hey, I wasn't ready to wake up yet." Sophie wrapped her arms around her slender waist and leaned back against the tiled wall, attempting to escape the chilly water.

"Baby, but you had some champagne on your skin. Let me make sure you're clean before I go." He reached for the body wash and poured some into his hands.

"Oh, in that case...by all means, proceed," She murmured and lifted her arms overhead, baring her beautiful body for him.

He massaged her skin in long slow circles, teasing around her breasts and down her slick skin.

"Don't miss this spot." She pressed his hand into her center. "Can you give this spot some extra attention?"

Oh yeah, Sophie wasn't afraid to show him what she wanted. He was ready for another round. She moaned and wiggled in closer, as hot and slippery as the shower was becoming. If this was committed love, he was sold.

After a long, hot satisfying shower, the last thing Nick wanted to do was head into the office and confront Heather, but he wasn't going to deal with her bullshit anymore. Nobody would upset Sophie if he could help it.

On the way into his office, he called his lawyer buddy, Paul, who advised him to give her a written thirty-day notice and offer her a severance package to leave now. Before he pulled into his parking spot, Paul had e-mailed over the paperwork.

When he arrived at his office, he stepped out of his car and mentally prepared for a scene. When had Heather morphed from an efficient employee to a nightmare?

Best-case scenario—she would be professional and would resign and leave today. Sure, he'd need to get his ass in gear to hire someone but that's what recruiters were for. Worst-case scenario—she took him up on the thirty days and did her job while looking for a new one and he'd be stuck with keeping her and Sophie separate.

He raked a hand through his hair and paused at the entrance. Damn it, for the last fifteen years, every building he designed, every concept he created, stemmed from the desire to pay tribute to his father's life by building a body of work worthy of the Pritzker. Besides his devotion to his younger sister, he'd purposefully blocked out any other entangle-ments, professional or personal.

Honoring the Morgan name had meant everything.

If Heather sabotaged him somehow, he could lose his legacy. His father's legacy.

But now, Nick understood another legacy his father had left him. That love was paramount. The love, devotion, and happiness his parents had shared and what he now shared with Sophie trumped any career accolade. He would protect Sophie and their love over everything else. Not winning the Pritzker didn't mean his life's work was for nothing—his buildings stood for themselves.

He'd risk it.

Entering the lobby, Nick called Heather's name through the open door to her office. She appeared in the doorway, sporting a bright smile. The moment she registered his mood, she schooled her features into an impassive mask.

"We need to talk. Come with me and have a seat." He turned and strode into his office.

She sat in the chair across from him. "What's going on Nick??

He powered on his computer, opened his email, and located the boilerplate thirty-day written notice legal document.

"I'm not going to beat around the bush, Heather. We need to discuss your position."

Her professional mask slipped, revealing a flash of panic in her eyes. "My position? Did I make an error on one of our projects?"

Suddenly, Nick noticed that her forehead was frozen and shiny. She looked like one of those women on reality TV-- plastic and hard. Funny, he'd never noticed before. What else had he misinterpreted about Heather?

He shook his head. Time to focus. "It's less about a specific error. Your performance is not satisfactory, your demeanor, and your recent behavior dealing with clients and the public in an unprofessional manner that doesn't reflect

CLAIRE MARTI

well on my firm. I don't think that you're the right fit any longer."

If Heather could have raised her eyebrows, they would have sailed off her motionless forehead.

"What do you mean?" Her mouth dropped open and she sputtered. "You've sent me to be your agent on numerous occasions. You've always praised my professionalism. What about the Pritzker? I'm your key representative on the nomination. This has to be a misunderstanding."

He held up one hand. "No misunderstanding. I can have my attorney compile a list of specific incidents. What is going to happen is this—you're on a thirty-day plan, effective immediately. During this time, your performance needs to be exemplary.

"If at the end of the thirty days, you turn around this pattern, we can discuss your future with Morgan Designs. If not, your employment will be terminated. If you would rather resign immediately, I'll give you three months' severance and provide you a glowing recommendation. Your choice."

Heather's mouth opened and closed, like a fish out of water.

*Too damn bad.* She'd fooled him. Once someone showed him their true colors, he didn't give second chances.

"Can we please discuss this? I'm sure I can explain whatever it is you think I've done. I've worked so hard to help you with the Pritzker, to raise your profile internationally. This is totally out of left field and—"

"I appreciate your efforts on the Pritzker, but that's in the past. I've made up my mind. This is how it is, and I think I'm being quite clear. I'll give you some time to decide." He stood, grabbed the thirty-day warning letter from the printer, and handed it to her. "Either sign this or give me your written resignation by the end of the day."

Heather grabbed the document and reached for a pen.

"Nick, I'm not sure what happened, and I'm very sorry you've gotten this impression about me. I'll do my best over the next thirty days to show you that I'm still the right-hand person for you and Morgan Designs. You have my word." She stood and handed him the signed agreement.

*Your word means shit.* He accepted the document with a curt nod and focused on his computer screen. For a moment, she remained in front of his desk, before leaving his office.

Nick slid the agreement into his briefcase. He pinched the bridge of his nose and closed his eyes. Well, at least she hadn't made a scene but what a shitstorm. He'd call Alyssa and have her reach out to a few of her recruiter friends and start the process of finding a replacement. Heather wouldn't last thirty days.

She wouldn't try to screw him over with the Pritzker, would she?

∾

"You want me to call who? And drive with you where?" Brandt said. "Has hell frozen over?"

"Shut up. I'll tell you all about it on the way up to L.A. Will you help me or not?" Brandt's uncle was a well-known jeweler up in L.A.

Last night, after Sophie had fallen asleep in his arms, he'd known what he wanted to do. Find an incredible ring to complement her beauty. To demonstrate his commitment to her. A symbol she was his and he was hers.

He rubbed his jaw and stared up at the ceiling. Had he been that much of a player his best friend thought he was joking? Although come to think of it, they'd both shared the dubious Player of Laguna title for the last decade. And Brandt was still rocking the title.

"Okay, okay. I don't know what planet you landed here from or what you did with my friend, but I'll call my Uncle John and tell him we'll be up this afternoon. He should be in his shop. Does Alyssa know?"

He groaned. "Shit, no, I haven't told her yet. Don't tell her. I will."

"Don't worry, we don't speak these days." Brandt's tone was abrupt.

"Why not?"

Brandt huffed out a breath. "Never mind. Fine, I'll go with you."

He smiled with satisfaction––his best friend never let him down. "I'll swing by in about twenty minutes."

"Well, at least drive the Beemer. That'll make the trip worthwhile. How about you let me drive her?"

Nick's buddy drove like a speed demon on a good day. "Hell no."

Brandt's tone turned sly. "It might help me remember to keep a secret if I got to take the wheel…"

"You're an asshole. Fine, you can drive. See you in a few." Nick never let anyone touch the wheel of his BMW, but now it seemed trivial to worry about it.

By some miracle, Brandt didn't kill them on the way to LA, despite his best efforts to break the sound barrier. Nick kept his focus on the prize: Sophie.

When they arrived at the jewelry store, Brandt's Uncle John was prepared with a velvet display showcasing several different rings. Swallowing down the punch of nerves in his gut, Nick examined the sparkling jewels.

Then he found it. The perfect symbol to complement Sophie's beauty. He waved Brandt over to see it.

"This is it, man. This is the one." Sophie would love it.

Brandt rolled his eyes. "Looks like an expensive piece of glass to me, but if you're set on it, it's your money."

Brandt's uncle wagged a finger at his nephew before turning his attention back to Nick. "Excellent choice. It's a three-carat Asscher cut in a platinum antique setting––one of a kind."

Nick ignored Brandt's snort. "Sophie's one of a kind. Yes, this is it."

"Give me a few minutes to clean it and box it up for you. I'll size it for you if it doesn't fit. Your young lady will be very happy." The lanky, white-haired man bustled away through a closed door.

Brandt smirked. "And you just made my uncle very happy with that little sale."

"Shut up. I can't wait until you meet the right woman. I'll be laughing all the way." Nick's lips twitched at the unlikely visual of his cynical buddy falling in love.

Brandt held up both hands and backed away. "No way will some chick put a noose around me."

Ignoring his idiotic friend, Nick whipped out his credit card and sealed the deal. Sophie would be able to gaze down at her hand and trust he wasn't going anywhere.

Ever.

When he'd learned about her ex's betrayal, the hurt she carried from having the rug yanked out from underneath her, had impacted him. Proposing sooner than later would demonstrate to her how serious he was. If he had anything to do with it, she'd never spend a sleepless hour again worrying about anything at all.

"WILL you slow the hell down? We need to stop and see Alyssa." Nick gripped the dashboard and glanced over at the speedometer and just how far above legal his friend was driving.

Brandt punched down the accelerator. "W-What? A-Alyssa?"

Why was his friend acting so out of character? "Damn it, slow down not speed up. Yeah, I need to show her the ring. She'd kill me for proposing without sharing it with her first. Hell, you've seen the ring, and you haven't even met Sophie yet."

"Can't you see her later? I have some stuff to do…" Brandt glanced over and caught his expression. "Fine."

Nick texted Alyssa and told her to meet him at Java Palace in twenty minutes. His always reliable sister agreed without question.

They squealed into the parking lot and swung into the closest spot. Nick grabbed the keys from his friend. "Okay, that's it, Speed Racer. My poor car will never recover. Learn how to handle the ladies with more finesse."

Brandt flipped him the bird and hopped out of the car.

They made their way into the quaint little coffee spot in Laguna. Somehow, despite Brandt's furious pace, his baby sister was already ordering at the counter. Alyssa turned with a smile, which disappeared when she noticed Brandt.

Nick hugged her, and after ordering their drinks, they made their way to a little Mexican-tiled wrought-iron table on the outdoor patio.

"Soo…what's up? What's the big news?" She leaned in toward him.

Brandt ignored them both and stared off in the direction of the ocean.

Showing was better than telling so Nick whipped out the black velvet box, opened the lid, and placed it on the table in front of Alyssa. She snatched up the box and squealed. "Ohmygod, ohmygod, ohmygod. No way. I can't believe it!"

She vaulted up from the table, and dragged him into a bear hug, her face glowing with joy. "I'm so happy for you. I knew you and Sophie were perfect for each other. I told you that. Ohmygod."

Brandt dropped his head into his hands and groaned. "Okay, okay, crazy Morgan family, you're making a scene. Sit down."

Alyssa glared at him. "Since when do you care about making a scene?"

"Whoa, kids, let's all sit down. What's up with you two?" Nick looked between them––what was with the tension crackling in the air?

Alyssa angled away from Brandt and focused on him. "Nothing. There's *absolutely nothing* between us. So, when are you asking her? Does she have any idea? Are you planning on getting married soon?"

"The way things are going, yes, I'll do it soon. Why wait?" A jolt of adrenaline spiked through his veins.

Brandt snorted. "Yeah, what possible reason would make you wait to propose marriage after weeks of knowing someone?"

"Have you even met her?" Alyssa snapped her head toward him, her eyes narrowed.

Brandt threw up his hands. "Hell, it's only been a few weeks—when would I have? This is nuts."

His buddy had a point. "I know it's fast. And I want you to meet her. Maybe we can all grab dinner later? Dude, you'll love her. She's incredible."

Brandt shrugged a shoulder. "I've got plans tonight. You remember that hot little redhead who works at the smoothie bar…"

"You never change. You're such a pig." Alyssa pushed back from the table.

"Hey, you two, cut it out. What's going on? This is my celebration, remember?" What the hell was up with his sister and his best friend?

Brandt turned toward him, a crease between his dark brows. "Sorry, man. Sure I want to meet her. Maybe later this week?"

"Cool. We'll make it happen."

Alyssa rose and hugged him. "Nick, I'm so happy for you, but I've got to run back to work."

His heart warmed. "Thanks. But if you see Sophie, don't breathe a word."

"Of course not. Let me know when it's a done deal." Without sparing a glance at Brandt, she sauntered away.

When they returned to the car. Nick took the wheel and glanced over at Brandt. "What's up, man? Didn't you and my sister used to be friends? Why are you being such a dick?"

"Sorry, man, nothing's up with Alyssa. We just don't really run in the same circles these days. Just getting used to the idea of the Player of Laguna taking on the ball and chain." He shifted his gaze out the passenger window.

*Whatever.* Brandt and Alyssa were adults––he wasn't going to stress over it. His own life was changing at break-neck speed and that's all he could handle. Sophie was spending the evening writing, so he had time to plan out his next steps.

Now he'd made his move and bought a ring, he needed to figure out how to give Sophie the most romantic night of her life. He swallowed down a flash of nerves––it wasn't too soon to propose, was it?

# CHAPTER 21

"So how's everything going with the book? With my brother?" Alyssa waggled her eyebrows.

Heat flooded Sophie's cheeks at her most recent memory of Nick. Which would be TMI for his sister. "Great, all of it is progressing really well."

"Well, thanks for taking a break and meeting me for yoga." Alyssa reclined back and tucked a strand of blond hair behind her ear. "For the record, I've never seen my brother like this with anyone."

Joy bloomed in Sophie's heart. "Really?"

"Let's just say he came by his player nickname honestly. Not that he was a total man-whore or anything, but he made it clear to anyone he dated that he wasn't interested in anything beyond casual." Alyssa's gaze grew distant. "After our parents died, he became so focused on taking care of me, and school, and his career, and I think he froze part of his heart."

"I can't imagine what that must have been like for you guys. I'm so sorry." She leaned forward and patted Alyssa's leg.

Alyssa shrugged a shoulder. "Yeah, it sucked. He's my only family, though, and I love him with all my heart. We're protective of each other, so if you aren't as crazy about him as he is about you, don't lead him on, okay?"

Sophie pressed one hand to her heart and her gut tightened—what if Alyssa found her to be lacking? Not good enough for him? "The feeling is definitely mutual. It's all happened so fast. I mean, I was planning on taking a man-break for a year and then Nick showed up. But I'm working on trusting my intuition and it feels right with Nick."

"Awesome, because I like you a lot and I love seeing him happy. I know we haven't had a chance to talk much about your family. You're an only child, right?"

"I like you, too. And I absolutely adore him. No, no siblings. I always wished for an older brother, though. It's just my mom and me."

"Your dad?" Alyssa arched a brow, in a gesture reminiscent of her brother.

"He left when I was five. I barely remember him." *Deadbeat*. And yeah, her people-pleasing personality––correction, former people-pleasing personality––and steamer trunk of abandonment issues could be tied to him.

Alyssa patted her arm. "I'm sorry to hear about your dad. At least you have your mom, right? Does she live in San Diego?"

"Yes, she's in San Diego, but we're just not very close. I'm sorry…I should be grateful to have her. I don't mean to be insensitive about your parents." And no way in hell will I be introducing her to either of you anytime soon.

"Hey, we all have our complicated family relationships. Please don't apologize. I've got my own trunk of issues, too but that's what therapy and yoga are for, right?" One corner of Alyssa's mouth quirked up. "Nick processes when he surfs, I think. But be gentle with his heart, please."

"I'm in love with your brother. I'd never hurt him. And it's funny, I feel you and I have known each other forever. It must be a Morgan trait."

"Me too. We Morgans are awesome. This is awesome." Alyssa glanced down at her watch. "I've got to run and get ready for work. I'm so glad we got to chat, and I'm thrilled about you and Nick."

Her spirits soared. "Me too. It means a lot to me that you're happy about us. Thanks for sharing more about your family."

They rose and headed their separate ways. Between yoga and her discussion with Alyssa, she was in the perfect mood to head back to the cottage for a productive day of writing. Telling Alyssa about her dad hadn't been as difficult as she'd anticipated. In general, she rarely discussed her childhood, except with a few of her closest friends, like Kelly.

At home, she showered, threw on an over-sized top, a pair of shorts, and brewed a pot of coffee. Leaving San Diego was the best move she'd ever made. That move had led her to take a chance to trust Nick. And she did trust him. Despite dating for less than a month, they were in love. He'd fallen in love with her—warts and all.

Would it matter to Nick she'd come from such a fragmented family?

A shudder ran through her at the prospect of Nick meeting her mom. No doubt Martine would embarrass her. Introductions could wait. Maybe next century? Complicated. It was all so complicated.

Part of the reason she'd left her job was to prove herself as a writer to prove to the world she could do it. To reinforce her self-esteem. On one level, she accepted she was worthy of love regardless of her accomplishments. On another level, her mom's critical attitude had hammered in her need for external validation.

If she peeked in the rearview mirror, there had been signs Doug had eroded her self-confidence. His controlling behavior, his intractable insistence on her having a "prestigious" job, and his scoffing at her dreams, to name a few.

Now she felt like a fool, she'd allowed him to manipulate her. She'd ignored her gut and tried to make it work, despite misgivings because she'd loved him. Or at least she'd loved the man he appeared to be––the guy deserved an Oscar. And after all of it, he bailed.

The coffee pot dinged, and she shook off the negative memories. No more getting mired in the past. Her heart and gut assured her Nick was her present. And her future.

An engine purred up the driveway. *Nick*. Maybe she had conjured him up to her doorstep. A little morning loving before diving back into her book worked for her. When had she become so insatiable? It was all his fault.

She crossed to the front door, yanked it open before he could knock, and struck what she hoped was a seductive pose in her oversized San Francisco 49'ers jersey.

"Sophie, I'm so glad you're home."

Her heart clutched and her coffee mug slid from her fingers and shattered on the doorstep. She leaped back and shoved the door shut.

Doug's hand caught the edge of the door before she could slam it in his face. "Sophie, please. Just give me ten minutes. Please."

"There's nothing you could say that I want to hear, so just get out of here." Tremors ran through her. She rooted her feet down into the floor. *Pull it together.*

"Please. Closure. Just give me ten minutes for both of us to have some closure. I think you'll be happy to hear what I have to say." Doug pressed the door further open.

Fury roared through her. "Closure? Oh, I got that on our wedding day, thank you very much. You can go to hell.

But how did you find me?" Who had given him her address?

His expression was contrite, his tone sincere. "Just hear me out and I'll tell you. Can I please come in for a few minutes?"

"Fine, ten minutes and that's it. Now how did you find me?" She stepped back and crossed her arms across her chest. Not that she cared about his bullshit, but she needed to know how he'd found her.

And perhaps a small part of her wanted to see him grovel. Well, maybe a gigantic part. Enjoying a little begging from the jerk before she booted him out of the cottage didn't make her a bad person, right?

"Follow me. And watch out for Zack. He still hates you." Sure enough, Zack perched on the couch, his back arched, his emerald eyes shooting daggers at Doug.

She reached the large picture window and turned to look at him. "You've now got eight and a half minutes."

He wore dark jeans and a snug black T-shirt. Objectively, the guy was tall, dark, and handsome. Except because she knew his soul was as dark as his outfit, nothing fluttered at the sight of him.

No attraction. No desire. Nothing.

An epiphany struck her like a thunderbolt. She'd agreed to listen to his story because she no longer loved him. Was truly over him. He no longer had the power to hurt her, at least not where it counted.

In her heart.

He flashed his old-school Tom Cruise smile, one of his arsenal of manipulative tricks. Funny now that she wasn't involved with him, he looked cheesy. Had she been blind before?

"Okay, first, tell me how you found me? Did Elizabeth give you my address?"

"Elizabeth? No. She was a total bitch to me," he narrowed his eyes. "No, it was your landlord's office manager."

Fury bubbled up in her gut. "My landlord? How did you find my landlord? And Heather gave you the address?"

He shrugged, as if hunting down your ex-fiancée was a run-of-the-mill occurrence, not borderline stalking. "Don't get hysterical. Does it matter? My old college buddy Ben saw you in downtown Laguna and texted me. It just took a little research after that to track you down."

"You're crazy, you know that? You ditch me on our wedding day after cheating on me for months, and you have the nerve to show up here? You had me. I loved you. You didn't want me. Your loss. You humiliated me in front of everyone."

She paused and inhaled a steadying breath. "I've moved on with my life, and I want you to get out. I shouldn't have let you in." She marched toward the door, eager to pound the final nail into the coffin of their shared past.

Doug didn't budge and he reached one hand toward her. "Hear me out. I've been in therapy for these last months. I was wrong, but it was my parents' fault––they screwed me up. I made a mistake and blew four years of commitment to you. You're the perfect woman for me. Give me another chance. We can drive to Vegas right now––I'm ready to marry you."

Sophie burst out laughing. Had Doug actually convinced himself his reality was real? More likely he'd practiced that facial expression in the mirror before he'd arrived.

The bottom line—he was delusional. Elope? Even if she were still in love with him, which thank the lord she was not, she wouldn't take him back. Cheaters didn't change.

Her feelings had changed. Bottom line––she loved Nick.

"You've got to be kidding." She doubled over now, bordering on hysterical. "I'm glad you've gotten some therapy because you need it, but this is about your ego. You're like a spoiled five-year-old. You only want me because you can't have me anymore."

He flinched, and something flickered behind his pale blue eyes. "Stop cackling like a lunatic. I know you're embarrassed. I'll make it up to you. You can trust me… I've got your ring." He reached into the front pocket of his jeans.

She straightened and pointed to the front door. "My ring? Have you listened to a word I've said? Forget it, Doug. I don't love you anymore. You should go."

His jaw dropped. Another bubble of laughter caught in her throat. Was she having an out-of-body experience? Standing outside of herself watching this ludicrous conversation unfold? Doug's gargantuan ego knew no bounds. He'd believed he could show up and spout his crap and she'd pop that meaningless diamond back onto her finger. *Unbelievable*.

When he didn't move, she brushed past him toward the door, and he grabbed her arm, spinning her to face him. She tugged, and he tightened his grip. His pupils dilated as he gazed at her mouth.

"Let go of me." She shoved at him with her other hand.

"No." He whipped her around, grabbed her other arm, and yanked her against his chest. He swooped down and kissed her before she could twist her head aside. He banded his arms around her, preventing her escape. She struggled, but he wouldn't budge.

Rage filled her and she bit down on his mouth. Hard.

He reared his head back, but his hold didn't soften. "What the hell! You bit me. What is wrong with you? Can't you feel our chemistry?" A flush rose on his neck and his breath came in harsh pants.

With a howl, Zack flew off the back of the chair and latched onto Doug's leg, digging his claws into his denim-clad thighs. He cursed and released her, pulling his arm back to strike her cat.

Adrenaline coursed through her, and she punched him in the face with all her strength. She stumbled backward, her hand throbbing, her breathing ragged. "Don't you touch my cat, you bastard."

He reached up and cupped his nose. "You broke my nose, you crazy bitch. You're going to end up a bitter old lady with fifty cats."

Nobody would accuse Doug of being handsome now. His sneer revealed his true colors. Ugliness dominated his face. Like The Picture of Dorian Gray.

"Living in a cave with two hundred cats would be preferable to another second in your pathetic presence. Get out, and if you ever come near me again, I'm getting a restraining order. Are we clear?" She pointed one shaking finger at him.

Doug backed toward the door and opened it with one hand, his rapidly blackening eyes spewing fire. "Try it and I'll press charges for assault. You invited me in. You kissed me."

"Get out or I'm calling the police." The adrenaline drained out of her––the dramatic scene plowing into her like a Mack truck.

Without shutting the door, he turned tail and hurried to his car. Tires squealed as he retreated down the driveway. A pathetic coward to the end.

Sophie sank to her knees in the doorway as Doug's car receded. Zack brushed up against her and settled in against her legs. Even his warmth couldn't dispel the chill enveloping her.

# CHAPTER 22

*A*fter a few moments, she dropped her head back against the doorframe and kicked herself for letting him inside. What had she been thinking? Was it her ego? The need to hear him apologize one more time?

Funny, it hadn't felt as good as she'd anticipated. In fact, an empty, disappointed void settled on her like a dark cloak. Tears wouldn't even form––not that the jerk deserved another moment of emotion from her. She'd wasted time pining away for something that never truly existed.

But one thing was apparent––her original plan to take a year being single to heal her heart was the correct one. Because although she was truly over Doug, she hadn't taken the time to grieve. To focus on herself, to rebuild her self-esteem, and to work on her dreams before getting involved with Nick. It wasn't fair to her, and it wasn't fair to Nick.

What if Nick had been with her when Doug stopped by? How would she explain that away? Sorry for the delusional ex-fiancé? Seeing Doug reminded her only a few months had passed since he'd deserted her at the altar. It was one thing to enter a new relationship with a carry-on bag but not a full set of luggage.

Carpe diem was one thing but was it really fair to Nick? He wasn't a rebound––her love for him was real––but the timing felt off now.

Zack butted against her legs. She lifted her head and cuddled her cat close.

And Nick's Beemer purred up the driveway. Perfect frickin' timing.

He opened the door and hurried over to her, his eyes hidden behind mirrored aviators. "Sophie? What's wrong? Who was that speeding down the driveway?"

Her gut clenched and the tiny hairs on the back of her neck lifted. If he'd stopped by five minutes earlier, he would have witnessed the nasty scene with Doug. What would he have done if he'd seen Doug kiss her?

Now her eyes filled, and she blinked away the moisture. Time to be strong, for both their sakes.

He reached one hand down and helped her to her feet. "Sophie, what's going on?"

"Let's go inside. We need to talk." She turned, headed to the couch, and licked her dry lips. "Have a seat."

Nick joined her but remained silent.

She exhaled a shaky breath and stared down at her clasped hands. "I think we should take a break."

"A break?" Nick's voice was neutral, not betraying any reaction.

She looked up from beneath her lashes and his expression was glacial. Her heart clenched. "Yeah, I just realized that we jumped into things really quickly and you know I'd planned on not dating for a year. It's all moving too fast. I need to focus on writing my book and you've got a lot going on with your firm, too."

Nick's eyes narrowed, his emerald eyes icy chips of glass. "Who was in that car?"

"It was my ex." Ex-asshole, that is.

His nostrils flared. "Really? The guy who cheated on you and dumped you?"

"Yes, I can explain—"

He surged to his feet. "Is that why you wanted to be alone last night? And he was here this morning with you still in your pajamas? What the hell, Sophie?"

"It wasn't what it looked like—he showed up unannounced this morning. Heather gave him my address, by the way."

His brow furrowed. "Heather?"

"Yeah. I'd been careful to make sure he didn't know where I'd moved, especially when I heard he was looking for me. But she told him, and he showed up, demanding..." She squeezed her hands together, digging her fingernails into her palms.

Nick's jaw was granite. "Demanding what?"

"He's delusional. He said he wanted to get back together and got angry when I told him to get out." Anger flared through her again.

Nick's face flushed red. "This doesn't make sense. The guy leaves you at the altar and then hunts you down to ask you to get back together? What aren't you telling me?"

Even though she was breaking things off, she didn't want him to have the wrong idea. Nick wouldn't believe the worst. Would he? He loved her. He trusted her. Would he give her the chance to explain?

"Nick, I'm so sorry, I'm telling you everything..." She stretched a hand toward him.

"You warned me you weren't over your ex yet, and I should have listened. And now you're dumping me right after he drives away?" With his face still carved in a grim mask, he pivoted away and crossed to the door.

She rose from the couch and hurried to the open doorway. "Nick, I *am* over him. I love you but I just need more time…"

"Stop." He held up one hand. "I got the message loud and clear. I'm out of here."

Without a backward glance, he reversed down the drive.

She locked the door, stumbled back to the sofa, and collapsed onto the cushions. Now the tears streamed down her face, sobs racking her body. What had she done?

Her best friend would know what to do. She grabbed her phone, Kelly picked up right away, and Sophie poured out the morning's nightmare events.

"Oh no, I wish you hadn't let that bastard Doug into your house. I can't believe Heather gave him your address. That woman is a piece of work."

She pressed her hands to her roiling belly. "I know, I know… It was a moment of weakness. It's so weird because I was with him for so many years, and now I feel like I never knew or even saw the real him. Believe me, if I could turn back time, I would have finished slamming the door in his face. Oh god, what do you think Nick will do?"

"Well, you told him you wanted a break, so he's got to be upset. Give him a little space. You know men tend to retreat to their caves when difficulties arise. He probably went surfing or something."

A staccato beat drummed in her temples. "Yeah, I wanted a break but if we don't clear the air and if he doesn't trust me, that might be the end of any chance we'd have of getting back together down the line."

"You're the most trustworthy person I know. He's angry and probably hurt. I'd give him time to process. Then call him and explain." Kelly paused. "But are you sure you want this break or are you just reacting to Doug's behavior? I think you need to spend some time reflecting too."

Sophie dropped her head back on the couch and closed her eyes. Yeah, she seemed to act impulsively because of Doug, didn't she?

"Hey, you still there?" Kelly asked a few moments later.

Sophie curled into a fetal position, spooning Zack. "Yes, I'm here. The break made sense before I saw Nick. I'm sure about my feelings for him but not about the timing, you know? But I'm afraid of giving him too much time to believe the worst. He is not a rebound."

"It's all going to work out. Give him some space and trust your feelings. I'm here for you, okay?"

"Thanks. I'll call you later." Sophie's heart cracked open.

Earlier she'd figured backing away from Nick would simplify her life but now? Not even close.

# CHAPTER 23

 $\mathcal{N}$ ick sped up the hill to his house; his vision clouded with red. Pain. Disbelief. Anger.

Last night, a flash of inspiration for the perfect proposal had come to him. Thrilled, eager like a little kid the night before Christmas, impatient to move forward, he'd decided to drop by and suggest the romantic trip to her in person. *Idiot.*

He'd reserved a romantic suite at his favorite winery in Paso Robles and arranged an afternoon of wine tasting, spa treatments, and an intimate dinner. After the perfect evening, he'd planned on waking up the next morning for a walk through the vines, where he'd propose. Sophie loved Paso and waiting until the morning to drop down onto bended knee would maintain an element of surprise.

Last night it had felt brilliant. Now? Not so much.

He parked in front of his house and smacked his hand on the steering wheel. *Shit.*

Rather than surprising Sophie with a sexy morning interlude, and telling her to pack an overnight bag, he'd been dumped.

Or duped. The ostentatious red sports car screeching down the road had been unusual but he hadn't suspected anything until he saw Sophie huddled in the doorway. He'd immediately tucked his emotions into the vault––the same way he learned when his parents died. The only example of true love he'd seen was between his parents.

They'd been killed at a young age—robbed of their happily ever after. He'd vowed to never allow anyone close enough to rip his heart out the way it had been when they had died. Until Sophie, he'd never considered softening his stance.

No woman had ever impacted him the way Sophie did. Then she was asking for a break, confessing that the jerk in the sportscar was the guy who'd bailed on her? She'd warned him she wasn't ready for a relationship, and he just couldn't listen. Even though he'd feared being the rebound guy and despite a persistent tingling in his gut, he'd forged ahead. Convinced he could change her mind. *Cocky idiot.*

Yeah, his first foray into love and commitment had been a disaster. Trusting her to be over her ex had been foolish. His own damn fault. And right now? He didn't want to hear her explanations. This time he'd listen to what she said first–– she wanted a break and he'd give her one.

What a joke. Here he'd trotted up to LA and bought a ring, eager to get married, have a family, and build a life with her. Nick stormed into his empty house. Something cracked in his chest, and the overwhelming urge to get away flooded him. Get far away.

He needed to get the hell out of Laguna. He'd go to Kauai and surf for a few days. Lose himself in the ocean, push the reset button.

Bury the last month and all things Sophie Barnes away.

Take a break, return and focus on work. Hell, he had more reason to fire Heather now if she had indeed given out Sophie's address. Finding a new office manager would take some time. But he'd deal with that nightmare later.

Brandt had been spot on in his assessment that he was nuts to get consider getting married. Staying unencumbered was safer. Easier. Maybe there'd be a little beach bunny in Kauai to help him drown his sorrows.

Although, for once, the concept held no appeal.

# CHAPTER 24

*W*here was he? Sophie shoved her hair away from her face and stared at her phone's dark screen. Nick hadn't responded to any of her texts and her phone calls went straight to voicemail. Almost twenty-four hours had passed since the scene at her cottage.

She had to clear the air. And make sure he believed her that he wasn't a rebound. Convince him her snap decision to take a break was a mistake. Yeah, she'd made that decision as a reaction to the confrontation with Doug. The minute she'd uttered the words, she'd wished she could take them back.

After a sleepless night, urgency drove her. She had to retract those words. See if they could start fresh, despite her blowing hot and cold. So much for giving him some space.

On the drive up to Nick's house, her entire body trembled. Despite the California sunshine, she was shivering, as if she were traversing the frozen tundra of Antarctica instead of a driveway in Southern California. She took long, slow breaths to soothe her nervous system.

But her yoga breathing wasn't helping her nerves. If she

was going to reassure Nick, she needed to maintain her composure.

When she pulled into his circular driveway, it was deserted. But he kept his cars in the garage. Maybe he was home. Ready to kiss and make-up. She snorted—unlikely. Although maybe he'd hear her out.

She stepped out of the car, squared her shoulders, and knocked on the front door.

Silence.

No wild barking. Not a peep from Bailey. Not a great sign. She banged again, but no giant dog and no Nick. *Crap.*

Once again, her life was messed up because of Doug. But even if Nick had zero desire to be involved with her now. She needed to assure Nick nothing had happened with her ex. He might not want to date her anymore but at least he'd know the truth.

So, off to his office she'd go. Where else would he be with his dog?

After navigating traffic on PCH, she parked in front of Morgan Designs despite not seeing his car. *Please don't let Heather be here.* The last thing she needed was that woman as her welcoming committee.

Sophie entered the royal blue office door. The moment she stepped into the foyer, Heather's door opened, and she appeared. *Of course she did.*

Dressed in a skintight pencil skirt, stilettos, and a fitted low-cut red silk blouse, the woman looked more like a socialite than an office manager. Her polish and poise made Sophie feel like a gauche, awkward teenager in comparison.

Once she'd decided to find him, she'd thrown on some yoga pants and a tank top, with her hair bundled up on top of her head in a messy, and come to think of it greasy, topknot.

Great.

Score one more point for Heather.

"Sophie. What can I do for you?" A smirk marred her face.

"Is Nick here?" Sophie clung to her thread of self-control. Screaming at Heather for giving her address to Doug would not help her find Nick.

"Nick? You sure are persistent chasing after him. He's not here." Heather's smirk deepened and she pivoted back toward her office.

Sophie gritted her teeth. "It's urgent. He's not answering his phone."

Oh god, was she really pleading with this icy bitch? Yeah, she was. She was *that* desperate.

"He's out of the office for a few days." Heather's tone was smug.

Sophie's pulse hammered in her throat. "A few days? Where did he go?"

"I'm not at liberty to share his schedule. If that's all, please shut the door behind you."

Sophie's energy drained and she turned toward the door.

"Oh, by the way, how was your reunion with your fiancé? He sure was a hottie," Heather called.

Sophie froze and her hands curled into fists. *Enough.* She'd had enough Heather.

The woman had the nerve to taunt her?

Spinning toward her, Sophie let loose. "Are you kidding me right now? You had no right to give out my address to anyone. No right. You are Nick's employee so stick to doing your job and stay out of my business. Do you understand me?"

Heather's jaw dropped, giving her an unpleasant expression like a cow chewing its cud. "I'll do whatever I damn well please you little bitch. I run this office and Nick needs me.

Now scamper back to San Diego where you belong." She flicked her hand.

Sophie had hit her limit, and she'd be damned if some plastic over-filled doll was going to talk down to her. No way would she shrink from this confrontation.

She barked out a laugh. "Bitch? Wow, you're so classy. Seriously, that's hilarious coming from you. You're just jealous. I'm sorry if I interrupted you searching the want ads since Nick has had enough of your unprofessional behavior."

Heather sputtered. Sophie took advantage of her momentary speechlessness to get in the last word.

"Yes, I know all about your thirty-day notice. Good luck with your job search and have a wonderful rest of your day." Sophie flashed an enormous grin and slammed the door behind her as she exited the office.

Oh. My. God. Did that really happen?

Would she wake up from this nightmare? In the last few days, she'd punched her ex-fiancé and won a nasty confrontation with Heather. Not to mention possibly screwed up the best relationship she'd ever had. At least she'd been able to articulate her feelings to Heather and make it crystal clear where she stood with Nick. Or used to stand with Nick.

Where was he? Although the last thing Sophie wanted to do was call Alyssa, at this point she no longer had a choice. Obviously, Nick hadn't been surfing at his local spot for the last twenty-four hours. He'd left town.

Without a word to her.

But could she blame him? She'd left San Diego when she was unhappy, so she understood the need for a fresh perspective. But her heart ached.

Up until yesterday, she'd been happy, convinced the tough patch in her life had ended. Following her dreams with her writing, falling in love with Nick, and starting fresh in a new town. Now it all seemed too good to be true.

Sophie drove down one of the side roads and parked facing the Pacific. The ocean always soothed her soul, and today she needed to cultivate some inner calm. Inhaling a fortifying breath, she called Alyssa.

"Hey Sophie, what's up?"

She struggled to keep her words even, normal. "Hi, I'm sorry to bug you, but I'm trying to track down Nick. He's not at home or at the office, and I need to talk to him."

"Really? That's odd. Did you check with Heather to see if he's off at a site?"

She cleared her throat. "Umm, long story, but she said he was out of town for a few days. I really need to talk to him—it can't wait."

Alyssa remained silent, and Sophie gazed down to see if she'd dropped the call.

"Alyssa?"

"What happened?" Alyssa finally responded. "He was in a great mood last time I saw him. But when he's upset, he usually takes off by himself. What's strange is that he didn't let me know." Concern colored Alyssa's voice.

Sophie's breath hitched—Nick hadn't told his sister he was leaving?

She gripped her thighs because they'd started shaking again. "Well, we had a misunderstanding and I need to clear it up sooner than later. He isn't responding to my texts and my calls are going straight to voicemail."

"Well, the only other person he may have told would be Brandt. He usually watches Bailey for him when he's traveling."

"Can you call him and ask if he knows? Please?"

Alyssa sighed. "Sure. Give me a few minutes and I'll call

you back. Do you want to tell me what happened? I might be able to help."

"I'd rather talk to him first. Just know that it was a mix-up, and I can clear it all up if I could just talk to him." Was she trying to convince Alyssa or herself?

They hung up, and Sophie nibbled on her pinky fingernail.

A few minutes later, Alyssa called back. "Well, I had to talk to Brandt, which is always annoying, but sure enough, Nick left Bailey with him. Brandt refused to tell me anything other than Nick asked him to watch his dog for a few days. I'm sorry."

"Well, could I call Brandt? Maybe he'd tell me?" No matter that she hadn't met the man.

"Trust me on this one, he'd never betray Nick's trust. Look, I don't know what went down, but I know he's crazy about you. He'll be back. You'll work it out." Alyssa's tone shifted from annoyed to comforting.

Sophie flinched at the phrase "betray Nick's trust" because that's what he believed she'd done. And there wasn't a damn thing she could do now but wait.

"Okay, thanks anyway." She stared out the windshield, but her vision blurred. The world appeared a dull grey.

Her stomach churned, and the pounding at her temples restarted with a staccato rhythm. The never-ending night-mare continued. That same sensation of paralysis—like when the monster was pulling you under the bed and you couldn't do a thing to prevent any of it. Helpless. Alone.

She'd promised herself she would never feel this way over a man again. But she loved Nick. Yes, she loved him and in her gut was positive he was the man for her. A man worth fighting for. And she would fight.

When she could figure out what to do next.

The beach, her usual haven, failed to comfort her because

now the waves reminded her of Nick and his passion for surfing. Time to head back to the cottage and regroup. She'd figure out a way to remedy this situation. Because she hadn't written a word in the past twenty-four hours and needed to get herself together.

When she arrived back at the cottage, it, too, reminded her of him. *Damn.* Come to think of it, everything about Laguna reminded her of him. He'd shared his quaint little town with her and in her heart, he remained intertwined with it.

Zack meowed and looked pointedly at his food bowls. Grateful for the distraction, she cracked open his favorite chicken and herring pâté and stroked his fur while he gobbled it down. Then, she curled up on the couch with him, comforted by his purring and pure, unconditional love.

She must have dozed off because the phone woke her up. She jumped up and ran to answer it. Zack squawked at being dumped unceremoniously from her lap.

Without glancing at the screen, she answered, "Nick."

"I'm looking for Sophie?" a woman's voice inquired.

Sophie coughed. "Oh, sorry about that. Yes, this is Sophie. May I help you?"

"It's Melissa calling from New York. I've got some good news for you."

She paced around the living room, willing her brain to engage. *Melissa Martin, the agent.* "Oh, hi Melissa, nice to hear from you."

"So I was at an industry event last night, and I was speaking to a colleague from another agency. We were discussing the never-ending search for the next big thing, and I mentioned you and your current project."

"Oh? What did she say?" Her hopes kindled.

"Well, she handles women's fiction, especially stories with a romantic twist, like yours. I told her your book wasn't finished, but she said you should query her and use my name."

Sophie gasped and pressed one hand to her throat. "That's fantastic, Melissa. Thanks so much for mentioning me. It makes such a difference to have a personal recommendation or contact."

"It does. And if you're flexible, I've got something more for you. She's flying to Los Angeles for some meetings today and said she'd love to meet you for coffee. Understand it wouldn't be for a formal pitch, but she likes to meet writers who she's considering representing. Just in case she decides to take you on once your book is finished."

"Seriously? Coffee tomorrow? Should I have a pitch prepared?"

"Well, like I said, she won't take a formal one, but it won't hurt to bring a synopsis because your story really does sound intriguing. Can you get up to L.A. tomorrow?"

"Absolutely." Sophie grabbed a pad and pen to write down the prospective agent's contact information. Hanging up the phone, she scooped up Zack and hugged him close.

She couldn't wait to share the news with Nick. *Crap*, Nick was gone.

He was the first person she wanted to share the news with, the first person she wanted to call. And he was MIA. Definitely did not want to talk to her.

If he would just pick up his phone and listen to her, she'd be able to clear up the situation in a few minutes. Or at least try.

Unable to settle her jangled nerves, Sophie set Zack onto his preferred spot on the couch and checked the yoga studio's schedule. If anything could give her some peace of mind, it would be some breath, movement, and meditation. At this point, she couldn't control Nick's behavior––ahem, she couldn't control anything at all except her own reactions.

She could also control how well she prepared for her agent meeting. Once she'd cleared her mind, she'd return and polish her synopsis. Even though she wouldn't be able to truly relax until she'd spoken to Nick.

He had to call her back soon, right?

# CHAPTER 25

*S*ophie shellacked a third layer of concealer on the purple rings beneath her puffy eyes. After tossing and turning all night, damage control was a must. No need for the agent to think she was a trainwreck.

Although trainwreck was an apt description.

Although today's meeting wasn't a formal pitch session, she wanted to feel her best when she met the woman. She stuck her tongue out at her pasty reflection. It was the best she could do under the circumstances.

Nick's radio silence hurt. At 3 a.m., she'd given up on trying to sleep and had written him a letter, pouring out all her feelings for him. Vulnerable, raw, and real. If after she returned from L.A., he still hadn't returned her calls, she'd give him the letter. What he chose to do with it was out of her control. Simply putting the words to paper had helped soothe her nerves. Mostly.

Thank god for her BFF. Kelly took the afternoon off and was meeting her in L.A. for a girls' night. Because right now, everywhere Sophie looked, signs of Nick overwhelmed her. From the empty pillow beside hers to the shower walls reminding her of hot, steamy sex, to the couch where they'd cuddled and watched movies.

Maybe a fresh environment would help shift her perspective. It couldn't hurt.

Time to focus on manifesting her dream of becoming a published author. Opportunity waited in Los Angeles. Smoothing down her crisp white blouse, Sophie squared her shoulders. She scooped up her overnight bag, assured Zack she'd return in twenty-four hours, and headed out the door.

Mourning the loss of Nick would have to take a backseat for now.

SOPHIE HUGGED herself as she skipped away from the café, a wide grin plastered on her face. The meeting with the prospective literary agent had gone better than she could have imagined. A New Yorker with a fashionable blond bob and a sharp wit, Jan Ashman had been encouraging after hearing her elevator pitch. Apparently, stories about starting over were always popular.

Although they'd only had time for a thirty-minute chat over coffee, she'd given Sophie her card and told her to send the query and first three chapters over once she'd completed her book.

Not that any guarantees came with Jan's offer to take her pitch, but she'd spoken to a real live agent who would at least consider her query. She'd savor the validation, thank you very much. Time to head to Shutters in Santa Monica–– Kelly was splurging on a room at the fancy hotel––and wait for her best friend.

Once she checked in, Sophie sat out on the room's gorgeous balcony and placed her computer on the teak table. Kelly wouldn't arrive for a few hours, so she could get in some new words. How could she not feel inspired by the ocean breeze, sunshine, and knowledge at least one agent would consider her book?

Ignoring the ache in her heart, she stuffed her feelings for Nick aside. Until they could sit down and have a discussion, brooding wouldn't help. Maybe she had overreacted asking for a break instead of simply asking to slow down. But right now, unless he called her back, she couldn't change a thing. She couldn't control his decisions, but she could control her own behavior. Cracking open the lid of her laptop, she began to write.

Three hours later, Kelly and Sophie clinked their champagne glasses. Time to toast her successful meeting and positive progress toward fulfilling her dreams.

Sophie shifted back in her chair and contemplated the twilight sky's streaks of lavender and rose. "I know it's just an agreement for someone to read my one-page query letter and first few chapters, but I'm on top of the world."

Kelly pointed a slender finger. "Don't downplay it. Having the chance to speak one on one with an agent is a big deal, regardless of the outcome. Remember that becoming a novelist is your dream and keep that in the forefront of your mind for now. Let's celebrate the wins and ignore the rest."

"You're right. My love life still stinks, but that's what compartmentalizing is for, right? Happy to focus on the bubbly and spending time with you." She sipped her drink.

"That's exactly what we're going to do tonight. But first, what are you going to do about Nick? Will you be able to stay in the cottage if you guys are finished?"

"Oh god, I don't know. I love Laguna and it already feels like home. It would stink to have to find a new place, not to mention I paid for the rent upfront. But I did tell him I wanted a break and he's given me that." Sophie smoothed a strand of hair away from her face.

Kelly leaned forward and placed a hand on her leg. "What do you want? Did you mean it when you told him you don't want to date him? You guys really seem to have something special, and I'd hate for Doug to screw your life up again."

"I just got scared. Everything happened so fast with Nick and just seems almost too good to be true. Factor in that bitchy office manager and how Nick reacted to learning Doug had been at my house…what do you think?" Worry swirled through her.

Kelly refilled their glasses. "Only you know what you're feeling but I've never seen you so happy. If it's the speed, just slow it down."

Sophie pressed a hand to her heart. "I love him, crazy as that sounds. But I'm scared and until he calls me back, it's all a moot point."

"I know you do, and he is obviously wild for you. You two will figure it out, day by day." Kelly gave her a reassuring smile. "But tonight we have this amazing hotel room and expensive champagne. Let's enjoy the sunset, go have an awesome dinner, and celebrate your victory toward becoming Oprah's next book club pick."

"I'll drink to that any day. Champagne first, fish tacos second, and then the world." Sophie lifted her glass. She'd be grateful for all the good in the present moment.

Even if that moment happened to be an illusory bubble created by her best friend and fancy wine.

Because no way could she contemplate the reality of living down the hill from Nick if he drove past her cottage every night with a different woman.

# CHAPTER 26

*N*ick dragged himself out of the pounding surf and flopped onto the sand at Polihale Beach, on Kauai's western coast. His bones ached, his muscles screamed, and his mind was blessedly blank. For the first time since the scene at the cottage.

Riding waves always put him in the zone, and he'd managed a few moments of peace. Mother Ocean always reminded him that life continued, no matter what. Life would continue for him no matter what, as well. Even if right now life without Sophie looked bleak.

Before he'd paddled out, he'd turned on his phone to ensure he hadn't missed any vital work calls. *Yeah, keep telling yourself that, dude.* Heather had texted to notify him she would accept the severance package and assured him she wouldn't interfere with the Pritzker. He wouldn't question her decision and frankly felt only relief. One problem solved.

He sat up and dropped his head in his hands. Sophie had left several voicemails and texts, but he didn't open them. Not ready to deal, he'd powered his phone off again. Did he even want to hear her explanation? Letting people close had never been easy for him and with Sophie flashing hot and cold...what the hell would he do if she said she'd changed her mind? Or if she was moving back to San Diego to reconcile with her loser ex?

How could he know if he was her rebound or not? Especially with her ex showing up at her house. At best, she'd confirm she wanted a break, and at worst she'd reconcile with the guy. Neither scenario worked for him.

If he reviewed the facts, he'd mooned over Sophie like some love-stricken teenager the minute Bailey had run her over. She'd told him point blank she didn't want to date anyone for a year. She'd warned him she wasn't ready. Several times. And he'd plowed over her objections, determined to win her over.

If it had just been sexual attraction, sleeping with her a few times would have been enough. Like with every other woman he'd been with before.

But Sophie had said she loved him. And he'd said those three words to a woman for the first time in his life. He'd said them first. He'd finally opened his heart, and she'd tossed it back to him. The fucking irony wasn't lost on him.

But he hadn't kept it physical because he loved everything about her––her compassion, her brilliant mind, her humor, her love of animals, her strength. He couldn't deny that Sophie Barnes was his one and only.

He ignored the sharp ache in his chest. Sophie Barnes had made it clear she didn't want him, and he'd take her at face value. Alyssa could handle any interactions with her for the cottage. Maybe it was a moot point, and she'd already moved back to San Diego with her ex.

*Screw it.* Nick ground his molars and scanned the perfect waves crashing onto the powdery sand. He'd flown to Kauai to surf and get his head on straight. Time to allow the ocean to put his life back into perspective.

Then, he'd return to Laguna and focus on what mattered––becoming one of the most successful architects of his generation and achieving the Pritzker Prize. Case closed.

A few hours later, Nick sat at the counter of his favorite local restaurant. Usually after a day in massive waves, he could scarf down enough for a JV football team. Tonight, he picked at his grilled Ono tacos, unable to muster an appetite to enjoy his food.

Despite his exhausted body, his mind raced on an endless loop. For the first time, the huge Hawaiian surf failed to clear his mind. Failed to soothe his heart. Failed.

Maybe he should get drunk. Maybe catching a buzz would help him forget about her. Why not? He took a long pull of his icy cold beer and thumped the empty bottle onto the counter and signaled the bartender for another round.

"Looks like you're celebrating. What'd you win?" A raspy voice asked from the stool beside him.

To Nick's left, a weathered, white-haired man with an overgrown mustache lifted his beer in a toast. The guy was a dead ringer for Sam Elliot.

"Ha, win? Not even close." Nick rolled his eyes and chugged half of his fresh beer in one shot.

"You visiting and couldn't catch any waves?" It seemed the old-timer wanted to chat.

Nick shook his head. "Nah, I ripped it up over at Polihale."

The man's lean face split into a grin. "Great spot, one of my favorites."

"Yeah, me too." At least he'd caught some killer waves today, despite his mood.

"So what could have you down in paradise if it isn't lack of surf?" The old guy waved a tanned hand.

Nick shrugged a shoulder. "I'm not down." *Liar.*

"Well, if you need an ear, I'm a great listener." He downed a mouthful of beer.

"I'm fine." Nick finished his drink in silence and squeezed his eyes shut. What the hell?

"So there's this girl…"

Old-timer chuckled into his beer and waved the bartender over. "Always is, always is. Let me buy you a shot. Joe, two tequilas."

Joe the bartender placed two healthy shots, a couple of limes, and two more beers in front of them.

Tequila wasn't his poison of choice, but again, why not? The hair on his arms prickled and he winced as the not-exactly-top-of-the-line liquor seared his throat.

Nick poured out the story to his new friend. "She's different. She's special…"

The man nodded. "So you ran off to lick your wounds. You only were with her for a little while, right? You're a handsome young dude––it shouldn't be tough for you to meet women. Write it off as a learning experience."

Nick's stomach twisted. "No, you don't understand. Sophie's unique. I've never loved anyone before. She's the first. She's the only one."

"I fell in love once, but I screwed it up good." The stranger glanced down, shaking his head. "Never saw her again. Dumbest move of my life."

"Maybe I should listen to her voicemails." Nick glanced at the phone sitting on the bar.

"Voicemails? She's been calling you? You gonna give her a chance to explain?" He pinned him with his gaze, dark eyes sharp.

Nick massaged the back of his neck. "She's left a bunch of messages."

"Don't be so stubborn you throw away something special because of your pride. If this girl is as special as you say, at least listen to what she has to say. Life's short. You know that saying right, carpe diem?"

Seize the day. "That's one of Sophie's favorite sayings. You're right."

He and Sophie had discussed carpe diem on their first date--the date he'd insisted on despite her reluctance. She personified the philosophy by moving to Laguna and starting over. She was courageous and strong and here he was, acting like a spoiled brat who didn't get his way.

Damn it. He loved her. He'd never experienced the pure joy and happiness he felt with Sophie. And he'd spent his entire life fighting for what mattered to him. So why the hell wasn't he fighting for her? For them.

Nick grabbed his phone and pressed play. He was a stubborn idiot--with each message, he couldn't deny the truth. If Sophie needed more time, he'd be waiting for her. Carpe diem didn't have to mean seize the day right now, it could mean declaring his intentions today and waiting for her to be ready because she was worth it.

"So?"

Nick patted his new buddy on the back, slapped some cash on the bar, and hopped off his stool. "So, you're right. Thanks, I appreciate it. I've got to get back home."

"Happy to help, happy to help. Good luck." His new best friend waved and turned back to his drink.

Nick hurried back to his hotel, booked a last-minute seat on the red-eye--the exorbitant fare was part of his penance--and headed to the airport. The sooner he could clear the air with Sophie, the sooner he could start proving to her that his love was real. And even though he was ready now--carpe diem and all that--he'd give her as much time as she needed.

If she didn't slam the door in his face.

⁓

BUZZING WITH CAFFEINE AND ADRENALINE, Nick pulled up in front of Brandt's house. He'd crashed hard on the plane when the hours in the punishing surf caught up with him. Now, he was eager to see Sophie. Maybe having Bailey with him when he returned would soften her up. Couldn't hurt his chances, anyway.

Brandt opened the front door before he could knock, and his sweet dog galloped out to greet him and slather him with kisses. Nick gave Bailey's floppy ears a vigorous scratching and glanced up at Brandt.

His friend leaned against the doorjamb; his arms crossed. "Back already? That was a quick surf trip."

Nick cleared his throat. "Yeah, it was. Thanks for watching Bailey."

"So you planning on sharing what this was all about?" Brandt cocked his head.

Nick adjusted his sunglasses. "Nope. Not right now anyway. Just had to clear my head."

His best friend's eyes narrowed. "Did you run off because of the woman? The ring wasn't big enough or something?"

"Dude, since when have you wanted to discuss my schedule?"

"Your schedule?" Brandt's lips twitched. "Since my buddy dragged me to L.A. to buy a diamond the size of his head and then ran off to Hawaii for a couple of days. Chalk it up to curiosity."

"Yeah, remember what they say about curiosity. Look, I'll fill you in later. Gotta run. Thanks again." Nick ushered Bailey to his car and escaped home before his friend could dig any deeper.

He settled Bailey into the house and showered off the

travel. Nick pulled on his favorite jeans and an ancient Cornell T-shirt for luck and headed down to the cottage.

Sophie's VW wasn't out front. *Shit*. He was ready to talk now.

He parked and knocked on the door. Silence. Where was she?

Damn it, he didn't want to have this conversation on the phone––that was why he hadn't texted her back telling her he was returning to town. No, when he saw her again, he needed to see Sophie's genuine reaction. Although it had only been a few days, it felt like a lifetime since he'd seen her beautiful face.

A car engine purred up the drive, so he jammed his hands in his pockets, attempting to appear nonchalant. When his sister's BMW drove up, he straightened, disappointment pouring through him.

Alyssa stepped out of her car and hurried toward him. "Nick, there you are. Where've you been?"

"Hi, I had to get out of town for a few days. Sorry I…"

She shoved him with a little bit too much enthusiasm. "Don't you *ever* take off without a word like that again. I was worried about you and had to call Brandt to chase you down. Imagine what you would have done if I'd just disappeared without and ignored your messages."

He held up his hands. "I know, I know—I screwed up. I'm sorry. It won't happen again. But I had to get away."

"Oh really? Why would you need space?" Her eyes widened. "What upset you? Or should I say who?"

He released a harsh breath and raked a hand through his hair. "You know it was because of Sophie. Do you know where she is? I need to see her. And what are you doing here?"

A crease appeared between Alyssa's brows. "She left town…"

"What? She moved back to San Diego?" Nick's throat tightened.

Alyssa patted his shoulder. "Calm down—she didn't move. She's out of town and asked me to come feed Zack for a few days."

Had Sophie given up on him already? Had he blown it by not returning any of her messages or calls? Was he too late? He sucked in a deep breath.

Alyssa's eyes filled with concern. "She did come looking for you and seemed pretty upset. Did you two have a fight? I've never seen you like this."

He flinched. "Look, I need to talk to her first. Please tell me where she went."

"I honestly don't know. I haven't heard from her. She said she'd text me when she had a return time. Why don't you call her and let her know you're back?"

"No, I need to talk to her in person. I guess I'll just have to wait." *Damn it.*

Was this how Sophie felt when he ignored her calls and texts? The longer they were apart, the faster his chances of convincing her he loved her and would wait for her plummeted.

What if he was too late?

# CHAPTER 27

The closer Sophie got to Laguna and reality, the tighter her chest became. When she pulled up to the cottage, Zack was perched in the front picture window. *Home.* At least for now. She grabbed her overnight bag and hurried inside to snuggle with her beloved kitty.

Time to settle in and write her book's next chapter-- where she created her own reality. She turned on the tea kettle and the doorbell chimed. Taking a cleansing breath, she crossed the living room. First, she peered through the peephole because she'd learned her lesson with Doug.

Her heart took a long tumbling roll in her chest--it was Nick.

She pressed one hand to her stomach and opened the door. Despite her galloping pulse, her heart warmed at the vision of him on the doorstep with a tentative smile on his gorgeous face.

"You're back." His voice was muted.

She nodded. "You're back, too." She couldn't prevent the tremor in her voice.

He cleared his throat. "Can I come in? We need to talk."

"Okay." She retreated a step and waved him inside.

The kettle whistled and she turned and hurried into the kitchen. "Do you want a cup of tea?" Although right now, whiskey would do more than Earl Grey to soothe her nerves.

"No, no, I just want to talk. Can we sit?" Nick followed her into the kitchen. Funny, the room hadn't seemed small before, but his clean beachy scent filled the space. The heat from his tall muscular frame was palpable.

She fiddled with the tea bag, poured the boiling water, and willed her fingers to stop trembling. "Let's go in the living room."

He pivoted and she followed him and perched on the edge of the couch. Safer to leave ample distance between them. She peered down into her mug as if the tea leaves would provide her with all the answers.

"Okay, hear me out. I've got a few things to share with you but first I owe you an apology…"

She lifted her head and met his gaze. "No, I owe you an explanation…"

Nick gave a quick shake of his head. "Me first, please. Let me get this all out or I'm afraid I won't. I'm not great at this."

She gestured with one hand for him to continue and wrapped both hands around her mug.

He exhaled a harsh breath. "I'm sorry I took off the way I did. I should have texted you back and let you know I was okay, but I just needed some space. I needed to cool off, so I headed to Kauai to surf for a few days and clear my head."

"Kauai?" Her eyes widened.

He scrubbed his hands through his tawny hair. "Yeah, it's one of the places where I can completely relax. Anyway, I was angry and frankly blindsided by your ex being here."

"That's what I need to explain to you. And--"

Nick held his hand up. "I'm almost finished. I'd come by to surprise you. To invite you away for a romantic night and

I get here and you're in your pajamas, your ex was here and then you tell me you want a break. I lost it, okay?"

She placed the mug onto the end table and turned to fully face him. Eager to share her side of the story, to clear the air, and maybe even take back the break idea.

Nick moved closer and took her hands in his large ones, his emerald eyes gleaming. "I listened to your messages, and I believe you. I've never been jealous before. I've never told another woman I loved her before. I'm sorry I bailed, and I won't do that again."

Sophie intertwined her fingers with his. "I'm so sorry. I was shocked to see him at the door, and then part of me wanted to hear him grovel and apologize. It only confirmed to me I was completely over him. But it also scared me because even though my heart is open and I love you, everything with you and me happened so fast. I reacted from fear of being shattered if we didn't work out. But I can't imagine not being with you. Can we slow things down a little bit instead?"

Nick tugged her onto his lap and banded his powerful arms around her. He buried his face into the hollow of her throat, murmuring her name.

She thrust her fingers into his thick, silky hair and held him close. "Does that mean yes? You want to be with me?"

He nibbled up the sensitive skin of her neck, leaving a trail of goosebumps, and captured her mouth. She moaned and parted her lips, swirling her tongue with his, savoring his minty breath. He slid his hands down to her hips, rocking her against his rigid length.

With a reluctant sigh, Nick lifted his head. "I absolutely want to be with you. At whatever pace works for you. We can go slow. But in the spirit of carpe diem…"

He released her and dropped to one knee and caught both her hands with his.

"Nick?" Her skin prickled, and the tiny hairs on her arms stood at attention.

He gazed deep into her eyes, pinning her in place. "The other day, I came by to invite you up to Paso Robles with me. I had a twenty-four-hour romantic getaway planned. I can't wait for that, though."

Her eyes widened, and the butterflies started beating in her belly. Her breath lodged in her throat.

He squeezed her hands and plunged on. "You are my everything. My dream. You make me want to be a better man. I've never loved another woman before. I love you with all my heart and promise to spend the rest of my life making you the happiest woman alive. And we can wait months or even years if you need them, but I hope you won't. Will you marry me?"

Nick reached into his pocket and pulled out a small velvet box, flipped it open to reveal the most exquisite diamond ring she'd ever seen.

Sophie released a shaky exhale and tears filled Sophie's eyes. This handsome, strong, incredible man was offering her his heart. And was willing to go at her pace.

Happiness burst through her heart, and tears of joy rolled down her cheeks. "Oh, Nick, I love you so much. Do you mean that you'll wait as long as I need?"

"It does. But is that a yes?"

She laughed through the tears. "I love that from the moment we met, you've been persistent and convinced I should be with you, no matter what. And yes, absolutely yes I will marry you Nicholas Morgan."

His beautiful lips curved upwards in a wide grin. He slid the ring onto her finger, and it fit perfectly.

He rose and pulled her up and into his arms. "I love you, Sophie. I hope you don't make me wait too long but knowing you're wearing my ring and declaring to the world you're mine makes me happier than I ever imagined."

"Let me show you how much…" Nick swept her into his arms and carried her to the bedroom.

Joy filled her and she tugged his head down for another kiss. Somehow she knew the wedding wouldn't be too far away. A certainty filled her that Nick was her one and only. Especially if he continued to carry her to bed.

# EPILOGUE

## SIX MONTHS LATER

*S*ophie typed her two new favorite words in the English language: THE END. Sure, it was on a crappy first draft of her novel, but it was finished. Now, she'd set it aside for a few weeks before the daunting task of a first round of edits. The manuscript would go through several rounds with changes with copy editors and proofreaders, but she'd completed an eighty-thousand word novel.

It wasn't like she'd ever finish the first draft of her first novel ever again. Actually writing a book was a milestone she'd commemorate. Time to celebrate.

Nick had booked a table at Nick's, one of their favorite local restaurants and Brandt and Alyssa were joining them for a congratulatory dinner. She closed her laptop.

Strong hands grasped her shoulders and Nick nuzzled her neck from behind. "I'm so proud of you, beautiful."

She rose and turned into his arms. "Thank you. I'm proud of me too. All the doubters can go on doubting because I did it." Triumph filled her.

"You're amazing. And I think we've got time for a pre-dinner celebration." He slanted his mouth across hers and her lips parted with a satisfied sigh.

She murmured against his lips, "Mmm, you would be correct. Our reservation isn't until 7. But Alyssa and Brandt are supposed to be here in twenty minutes for a pre-dinner drink, right?"

He lifted his head, his green eyes heavy-lidded. "Correct. Maybe we'll have to wait until after dinner because I've got one more thing to ask you."

"Yes?"

He clasped her jaw in one hand and gazed into her eyes. "We've been engaged for three months now and I'm hoping you're ready to move in with me and set our wedding date."

Joy sparked through her. Although they had spent almost every night together since their engagement, she'd kept the cottage. Just in case. But now the timing seemed right. She'd finished her book. Each day they grew closer, and her heart simply knew Nick was her ride-or-die person. And she was his.

"Yes and yes." She threw her arms around his neck.

He grinned and twirled her around the room. "Tomorrow?"

She laughed. "Maybe to move in, but I want a wedding so that will take a while."

He captured her mouth, and heat bloomed low in her belly. She'd never get enough of Nick. She pushed him down onto the sofa and straddled his lap.

Maybe they could pull off a quickie before Brandt and Alyssa arrived. "We've got fifteen minutes, right?"

He caught her hips and rocked her against his rock-hard arousal. "I'm game."

The doorbell rang, followed by the door opening. "Hey guys, I brought bubbly," Alyssa called.

Sophie shifted off Nick's lap and landed on the sofa beside him. "You're early."

Alyssa's eyebrows rose and she strode past them to the kitchen. "You two are out of control. I'm popping the cork. I need a drink if I'm going to spend the evening with Brandt and you two making out the whole time."

Nick adjusted his pants, rose, and held out a hand to her. "Rain check."

She accepted his hand with a smiled for the love of her life. "Deal. And are those two still not getting along?"

Nick held up one finger to his chiseled lips. "Shh, let's avoid that situation completely. Let's go tell her you're moving in and we're setting a date."

"Knock, knock," Brandt opened the front door. "Sorry I'm early but I need a drink."

Sophie and Nick looked at each other and burst out laughing.

"What?" Nick's best friend arched one dark eyebrow. "What's so funny?"

Nick recovered first. "Nothing. Come on in. We've got some more news and don't need to repeat it twice."

The loud pop of the champagne cork sounded from the kitchen. Alyssa appeared in the doorway, clutching the bottle. "What's so funny?"

The minute she caught sight of Brandt, Alyssa's smoky blue eyes cooled. "Oh, you're here."

"Yeah, I'm here." Brandt remained rooted to the spot.

Sophie looked between them; her curiosity piqued. Over the last few months, she hadn't seen Brandt and Alyssa together and the tension simmering between them was palpable. What was their deal?

Nick gave Brandt a questioning glance. "Let's pour that champagne. Sophie finished her first book and tonight is all about her."

Alyssa's expression cleared and she pivoted back toward the kitchen. "Of course it is. I've got the glasses ready."

Alyssa poured them all a glass of champagne and stayed on the opposite side of the kitchen island from Brandt. She raised her glass. "To Sophie, our future bestselling author."

They clinked glasses and sipped. Warmth filled Sophie as she looked around the small room. "You guys don't know how much this means to me and tonight is doubly sweet because Nick and I have some news."

"More news?" Brandt asked.

Nick wrapped one arm around her and pulled her close to his lean muscular frame. "Sophie's agreed to move in with me and we're going to set a wedding date."

Alyssa's gorgeous face broke into a wide smile. "That's amazing news. Congratulations on everything. I'm really happy for you both."

Brandt lifted his glass again. "Congrats."

"And I want you to be my best man, okay?" Nick turned to Brandt.

Brandt's mouth dropped open. "Yeah?"

"Of course. Who else? Will you do it?"

Brandt shrugged a shoulder and if Sophie didn't know better, she'd think he was blushing. "Yeah, I'd be honored."

Sophie turned to Alyssa. "And will you be a bridesmaid?"

Alyssa nodded enthusiastically. "Of course, I will."

"And since Kelly lives in San Diego, I may need to lean on you and Brandt a lot, okay?" Sophie glanced between them again.

Brandt's nostrils flared and Alyssa stiffened. Something was brewing between Nick's best friend and his little sister.

# ACKNOWLEDGMENTS

This version of *Second Chance in Laguna* comes to you eight years after I wrote the original book. When I received my rights back from my former publisher, I was excited to update and edit Nick and Sophie's story to match my original vision. Imagine my surprise when I saw just how the "light edit" I envisioned became a virtual rewrite. The black moment and ending are new. Areas which weren't fully developed are--I hope--all keeping the original story as intact as possible.

This story was my first and as I write these acknowledgments, I've now written fifteen more novels and novellas. What a ride! Reading the story again was humbling--I've grown so much as a writer, but I still love Nick and Sophie and I hope you do too.

I want to thank my wonderful beta readers and critique partners. Kay Bennett, Lacy Pope, Joanna Kelly, Leslie Hachtel, April Fink, Megan Randall, and Megan Camp who all helped with the original story and believed in me. You each helped me more than you could imagine. I appreciate your time and opinions.

Finally, to Todd for your unwavering belief in me. I love you. And, finally to my furry kids: Lola, Beau, Josie, and Daisy, thanks for providing me daily laughs and all the cuddles.

# ABOUT THE AUTHOR

Claire Marti is an award winning and *USA Today* Bestselling author of swoonworthy Contemporary Romance novels set in Southern California, including the Pacific Vista Ranch series and spin-off California Suits series. She lives in San Diego with her husband, silly dog, and three clever cats.

Claire started writing stories as soon as she was old enough to pick up pencil and paper. After graduating from the University of Virginia with a BA in English Literature, Claire was sidetracked by other careers, including practicing law, selling software for legal publishers, and managing a non-profit animal rescue for a Hollywood actress.

Finally, Claire followed her heart and now focuses on two of her true passions: writing romance and teaching yoga.

# ALSO BY CLAIRE MARTI

**Pacific Vista Ranch Series**

Nobody Else But You

The Very Thought of You

For The Love of You

Wrapped Up with You

The Wonder of You

**California Suits Series**

Hotel King

Wine Country King

Monterey King

Holiday Queen

Palm Springs King

**Romance in Laguna Beach Series**

Second Chance in Laguna

At Last in Laguna

Sunset in Laguna

Ingram Content Group UK Ltd.
Milton Keynes UK
UKHW010735170723
425272UK00001B/12